2/11

Henriette Delille

Henriette Delille

Rebellious Saint

**By Elsie B. Martinez
and Colette H. Stelly**

Illustrated by Phyllis Reppel

PELICAN PUBLISHING COMPANY
GRETNA 2010

*The word "Pelican" and the depiction of a pelican
are trademarks of Pelican Publishing Company, Inc.,
and are registered in the U.S. Patent and Trademark Office.*

Library of Congress Cataloging-in-Publication Data

Martinez, Elsie.
 Henriette Delille : rebellious saint / Elsie B. Martinez and Colette H.
Stelly ; illustrated by Phyllis Reppel.
  p. cm.
 ISBN 978-1-58980-839-3 (hardcover : alk. paper) — ISBN 978-1-58980-
841-6 (e-book) 1. Delille, Henriette, 1812-1862—Juvenile literature.
2. Sisters of the Holy Family (New Orleans, La.)—Biography—Juvenile
literature. 3. Sisters of the Holy Family (New Orleans, La.)—History—
Juvenile literature. I. Stelly, Colette H. II. Reppel, Phyllis. III. Title.
 BX4496.7.Z8M37 2010
 271'.97—dc22
 [B]
                          2010023192

*Stained-glass windows of Mother Henriette Delille at Saint Louis Cathedral in
New Orleans, Louisiana, designed by Ruth Goliwas
Jacket photography by George Reppel*

Printed in the United States of America
Published by Pelican Publishing Company, Inc.
1000 Burmaster Street, Gretna, Louisiana 70053

To our beloved husbands,
John Luiz Martinez
and René James Stelly,
who both died while we were writing this manuscript

Contents

Acknowledgments

Many friends and companions read our manuscript in its various stages of development and offered valuable suggestions both before and after Hurricane Katrina, which delayed our work considerably. We are most grateful to Adolfo Anderson; Jack Belsom; Mary Lee Burke; Helen Callaghan; Jean Cassels; Liliane Crété; Marie Louise Davidson; Laura Dragon; Debbie Eggers; Marjorie Gehl; Julie Gonzalez; Sister Doris Goudeaux, SSF; Angela Kelly; Maria McDougal; Françoise Rodary McHugh; Lester Perryman; Peter Rogers, SJ; Sarah Smither; Bernadette Szost; and David Walker.

We also acknowledge with gratitude the information afforded to us by the manuscripts "Violets in the King's Garden," a history of the Sisters of the Holy Family of New Orleans by Sister Francis Borgia Hart, SSF; "Henriette Delille: Servant of Slaves," by Virginia Meacham Gould and Charles E. Nolan; "Servant of the Slaves: The Story of Henriette Delille," by David R. Collins; "Henriette Delille: Servant of Slaves, Witness to the Poor," by Cyprian Davis, OSB; and "Religious Pioneers: Building the Faith in the Archdiocese of New Orleans," edited by Dorothy Dawes and Charles Nolan.

Chapter 1

Dead Dog and Slaves for Sale

New Orleans, 1823

The downpour that had begun before dawn finally stopped around mid-morning. Henriette Delille ran out the front door of her house, down the steps, and on toward Barracks Street just as her friend Juliette was turning the corner. Henriette waved and rushed to meet her.

"Let's go," she cried and took Juliette's hand. Yesterday they had decided they would go to the French Market to watch the fishermen bring in their catch. Henriette hoped they'd have some turtles so her mother and dear old Nanou could make turtle soup. It was her favorite dish.

They laughed as they gingerly crossed the street, holding their skirts above the muddied cobblestones. They picked up their pace and hurried to the corner, turned toward the French Market, then stopped short at the pitiful sight in the middle of the street. Both girls gasped.

"Oh, no," cried Henriette.

"What's the matter with you girls? Haven't you ever seen a dead dog before?" said a skinny little boy standing over the lifeless body.

It wasn't unusual to find a dead animal in the streets of New Orleans, even right in the middle of the French Quarter. Henriette and Juliette were used to coming across the carcasses of cats and dogs, sometimes pigs or sheep, and once they saw the body of a cow on Dumaine Street. But this animal was one Henriette knew well, a pretty little tan and white spaniel that belonged to her neighbor, Mme Hymel.

"He's dead all right," said the boy, poking the dog with a long stick.

"Oh, it's Pitout!" cried Henriette. "Poor Mme Hymel, she's going to be so sad. Stop poking him," she said sharply to the boy. "We have to take him home to Mme Hymel."

"We do?" asked Juliette. "How can we? We can't carry him." Henriette looked at the boy. "Maybe you can help us," she said.

He frowned at Henriette, threw his stick away, then turned and disappeared down the street.

"Well, it looks like we'll have to do it ourselves," said Henriette as she walked over to the dog, leaned down, and lifted up one of his paws. A mud puddle beside him was streaked with blood.

"He's got blood all over him," commented Juliette.

"He must have been hit by a carriage or maybe kicked by a horse," said Henriette sadly as she stroked little Pitout's head. "I think Mme Hymel will want to bury him, don't you?"

"I guess so. Maybe we better go back and tell her about him and she can come get him."

"Mme Hymel is old, Juliette, she can't even get around very well. She won't be able to bury him. We'll have to help her. Do you think we could say some prayers for him?"

"That would be nice. Do dogs have souls, Henriette?"

"I don't know. God made them so he must love them. Besides, I'd like to have dogs in heaven, wouldn't you?"

"I suppose. Maybe we should ask Sister Ste Marthe about it." Sister Ste Marthe was their teacher at the St. Claude School.

Just then two men on horseback turned the corner and shouted at the girls, "Get out of the street, you silly girls." They pulled up their horses and one of them asked, "What in the world are you doing with that dead dog?" He looked closely at Henriette. "Aren't you Pouponne Diaz's little girl?"

"Yes, sir, I'm Henriette Delille." She curtsied and added, "This is my friend Juliette."

"I see. How old are you, Henriette?"

"I'm ten, sir, almost eleven."

"Well, this is no place for you, in the middle of the street with a dead dog. You'd better go home." He pulled his horse over as another horseman rode by sending pellets of mud in their direction.

Juliette backed away, trying to brush the wet stains from her gingham dress. She grabbed Henriette's arm as she turned toward home, but Henriette pulled away. She looked up at the gentleman and pleaded, "Won't you please help us take Pitout back to Mme Hymel? He's her dog. She's our neighbor. We want to bury him in her patio."

The gentleman muffled a chuckle and looked at his companion. "What do you think, Pierre? Have you ever had such a strange request before?"

"Well, we're early for the hunt," replied Pierre with a shrug. "Why don't we oblige?" He reached into his pack, pulled out gloves, and put them on. Dismounting, he picked up the dog by the tail and placed him in his empty hunting bag.

"Good, Pierre. Off we go then. Girls, you lead the way."

And so, in procession with Henriette and Juliette in the lead, they arrived at Mme Hymel's Creole cottage. The girls took Pitout from the riders with many thanks and deep curtsies. They each picked up a paw and then dragged him to the patio behind the house. Hearing voices, Mme Hymel stepped out of her back door, started to smile at the girls, then gasped as she saw her darling dog. *"Ah, mon cher Pitout!* What happened?"

"A carriage must have hit him," said Henriette, looking forlorn. "We're so sorry. We found him in the middle of the street."

"Pitout was so old, I guess he couldn't get out of the way in time," sobbed Mme Hymel, tears streaming down her cheeks. She bent down and gently cupped his head in her hands. "He was such a good dog."

"We'll help you bury him," said Henriette. She looked around the patio. "How about under that banana tree?"

It was easy to dig up the earth, softened by the night's rain. After the burial they staked a small cross atop Pitout's grave, quickly rubbed their muddy hands on their skirts, and all together said the Our Father. It was the first time Henriette presided at a funeral, but it would not be the last.

Later that morning, after consoling Mme Hymel as best they could, the girls headed again for the French Market. As they neared Decatur Street, they heard loud music and saw a crowd forming near the fishermen's stalls. Everyone was looking up at a makeshift platform in the middle of which stood a large wooden chair.

"Look!" exclaimed Juliette, pointing to the platform. "What are they doing to that man?"

Two men were pushing a third one into the chair as a small brass band played louder and louder. The crowd began to cheer.

"Oh, it's the dentist," said Henriette. She winced as she raised her hand to her jaw. "I just hate this. Let's go see the crabs." She pulled Juliette by the arm, but Juliette resisted.

"I want to see what's going to happen," she said.

"Haven't you ever seen the dentist? It's too awful to watch."

Just then, one of the men pulled open the mouth of the man in the chair while the other held his arms down. The musicians played a loud fanfare, almost drowning out the screams of the patient, whose feet kept jerking up and down. The dentist reached in, then yanked and jerked till he extracted a tooth. Juliette gasped but watched in fascination as the dentist turned to the crowd and triumphantly displayed the culpable tooth. Many of the men applauded and slapped their legs, laughing heartily. The music finally died down and the crowd began to disperse.

"Does that happen very often?" asked Juliette, her eyes wide.

"No, thank heaven. Just when the dentist shows up and some poor person has such a terrible toothache he can't stand it."

Their spirits lifted as they entered the market, skirting their way through swarms of adults buying and selling their wares. They loved coming here. It was the hub of activity for city dwellers who came daily to purchase fresh produce and other *comestibles*. The strong aroma of freshly caught seafood soon assailed their nostrils and they watched as fishermen unloaded mounds of fish, squid, baby octopi, and shrimp onto the tables, then they dumped hampers of crabs and crawfish into wicker bins below.

"I love the crabs, don't you?" Henriette laughed as she teased a large crab into snapping his claws at her fingers. She quickly drew them away.

"Don't do that, Henriette," admonished Juliette with a shudder. "You're going to get pinched."

"Oh, I'm quicker than they are," Henriette said confidently, waving her hand back and forth, causing several crabs to snap and hook their claws on the side of the cage.

"And look, they have lots of turtles." She pointed to another table where several green turtles were lying helpless on their backs, their feet moving feebly back and forth. "I'm going to tell Maman when we get home. I bet we have turtle soup tomorrow."

Juliette took one glance, then looked away. "They sure are stinky, aren't they?"

"Phooey . . . yes, they are! Let's go to the vegetable stalls. There's always a lady there that sells rice cakes and it'll smell much better."

They walked along the arcade, passing customers bargaining loudly with vendors, till they came to the vegetable stalls. Piled high on two crude wooden tables was a kaleidoscope of bright colors—yellow squash, green peppers, red and yellow onions, carrots, huge heads of cabbage, strings of white garlic pods, purple eggplants, and bunches of bright green parsley. After passing the vegetables, they noticed a sweet aroma, emanating from the lap of a wrinkled old mulatto woman sitting between the tables and holding in her lap a basket of crisp, warm rice cakes. Beside her a sign proclaimed, *"Calas Tout Chaud."*

"Don't they look delicious," cried Henriette, her mouth watering. "Do you have any coins?"

"No," said Juliette with a disappointed shake of her head. "I don't either."

Just then Henriette heard someone call her name. She turned and a smile lit up her face as she made a deep curtsy to the brown-robed figure before her.

"Père Antoine," she cried. "I'm so glad to see you. My *maman* said you were away—and we missed you."

The legendary priest of St. Louis Cathedral patted Henriette on the head, saying, "My, Henriette, you're growing up too fast. But you still like the calas, I see. And Juliette, too, no doubt."

Lifting his robes, he took a few coins from his pocket as the old woman quickly bowed her head to the priest then handed each of the girls a rice cake. The girls expressed their profuse thanks between bites as Père Antoine turned to leave.

"Henriette, be sure to give my best regards to your dear *maman* and to Jean and Cécile also," he said, waving his goodbye.

"Oh, he's so wonderful," said Henriette. "My *maman* says he's a true saint."

They were silent for a few moments, licking their fingers as they finished the last bit of the calas.

"What should we do now?" asked Juliette.

"Let's go to my Oncle Félix's grocery. He might give us another treat," Henriette laughed.

The girls walked toward Esplanade Avenue, skipping along and stopping a couple of times at the market's archways, where Choctaw Indian women displayed beautifully woven baskets, colorful pottery, and bright strings of beads. When they reached Esplanade, they stopped short and looked across the street to where a group of blacks and mulattoes— men, women, and children—were lined up in front of a two-story house. The children were clinging to the women's skirts. Both girls knew what this was: a line-up of slaves for sale. They were all dressed in neat, clean clothes and stood silently for inspection by possible buyers.

"Look at the two men with the big top hats," said Juliette. "They look like undertakers."

She and Henriette looked solemnly at the group. Henriette suddenly cried out, "Oh, I think that's old Joseph." She grabbed Juliette's arm. "That one with the hat at the end of the line," she pointed. "His owners asked Maman to nurse him last year when he got sick with pleurisy."

"Who are the owners?"

"The Landrys. They live right around the corner from us. But what's he doing here in this line? Let's ask my Oncle Félix. I'm sure he'll know."

She waved at Joseph and tried to catch his eye, but the old fellow never lifted his head or took his eyes from the ground.

"Well, let's go," she said finally with a sad shake of her head.

Their exuberant mood was gone. No skipping now, their steps were dragging, their faces pensive as they turned and continued down the block to Uncle Félix's store. A large sign above the entrance proclaimed, "Félix Delille Grocery and Emporium."

"I've never been here before," said Juliette. "Is M. Félix your real *oncle* or do you just call him *oncle?*"

"He's my real *oncle.*" Henriette paused a moment. "He's my father's half-brother."

"Really?" said Juliette in surprise. "Will your father be at the store?"

"Oh, no, no. He doesn't live in the city, but my Oncle Félix sees him sometimes. Once in a while he gives *mon oncle* something for me; last time he was here he gave me a pretty comb."

As they approached the entrance, Uncle Felix's young slave, Jacques, came out carrying a large sack on his shoulder. "Hi, Miss Henriette," he said cheerfully. "I'se bringin' dis sack o' flour to your *maman.* Ah bet Nanou's gwine make a lot o' beignets for y'all."

"I sure hope so, Jacques," said Henriette. "Is *mon oncle* here?"

Just then Uncle Félix looked out the entrance and smiled. He wore a white apron and had a pencil tucked behind one ear.

"Ah, Henriette, come in. I see you have someone with you."

"*Oui, mon oncle,* this is my friend, Juliette. Her folks are from the islands."

Juliette smiled shyly and curtsied.

"And what can I do for you young ladies today?"

"Oh, the saddest thing. Do you remember old Joseph whom Maman nursed last year when he came down with pleurisy? Well, Juliette and I were just over on Esplanade and . . . there's a slave market there and Joseph is one of the ones for sale! He's wearing a big top hat and he looks so sad."

"I didn't know Joseph was in that lot. I guess he's the one the notice says is old and not strong. Look up there." He pointed to a sign tacked to the side of the grocery next to the door.

Henriette and Juliette walked over, stood on tip-toe and read:

NOTICE
Saturday, April 15, 1823
Newly arrived shipment of Negroes from Virginia and Maryland.
Cheap. At my old stand on Esplanade near Chartres Street.
Most in very good condition. Also one elderly slave
can be used as house servant. Very cheap!

"Elderly . . . that must be Joseph all right. Why would the Landrys want to sell him?"

"Oh, I guess he's just too old to do very much any more, Henriette. I don't think he ever came back from that pleurisy he had."

"What will become of him? No one will want him, he's so old. The notice says he's very cheap." Henriette paused and then looked imploringly at her uncle. "Do you think you could buy him, *mon oncle?* He could help a little in your store."

Uncle Félix laughed, but his expression changed to sympathy as he saw that Henriette was close to tears. "I'm sorry, Henriette," he said, putting his arm around her. "Poor old Joseph couldn't help me enough. Perhaps someone else will buy him as a house servant. I'll tell some of my customers about him. He's a nice old man."

Henriette looked down with a sigh and then looked up into her uncle's eyes. "I wish I had some money; I'd buy him." Her uncle shook his head and shrugged his shoulders, then hugged Henriette gently to him and steered her into the grocery. "You girls come on in and we'll look around and find something nice to take your minds off old Joseph."

Juliette followed as Uncle Félix went over to a shelf bulging with stalks of sugar cane. He pulled a stalk down, took a knife from his belt, and cut two pieces, handing one to each. "Here, suck on that for a while. It'll make you feel a little better." The girls slowly began to chew on the cane, making small slurping sounds as they licked the juice that ran down the stalk.

Uncle Félix went behind the counter, into the back of his store, and came out with a handful of lemons. "I have these for your *maman*, Henriette. She'll be mighty happy to get them." He put them into a small burlap sack and handed them to his niece.

"Thank you. We haven't had lemons in a long time."

Uncle Félix laughed. "You tell her to make you some delicious lemonade or even better, a nice lemon custard."

Henriette swung the bag of lemons back and forth, looking around the store, then at her uncle. "Suppose no one buys Joseph. What will happen to him?"

"Well, I guess the Landrys will just have to keep him and try to sell him another time. But don't worry about old Joseph, Henriette. He'll be all right. I'll talk to the Landrys about him, maybe send them an extra sack of flour or sugar, ask them to look after him."

Henriette's face brightened. "Oh, thank you, Oncle Félix. You're so good." And she threw her arms around his waist.

He patted her head. "You're a funny one, Henriette. Now, you'd better get on home or your *maman* will be out looking for you."

The girls headed down Bourbon Street, still sucking on their sugar cane.

"Your *oncle* is so nice," said Juliette. "He's your father's brother you said?"

Henriette hesitated. She frowned a little, thinking of what to say. "You know, we see Oncle Félix all the time. But since my father doesn't live in the city, we only see him a few times a year." She paused, remembering how special his visits were. "Maman gets so nervous when he comes. She makes sure the house is spic and span and puts flowers in all the rooms and Nanou cooks all his favorite dishes. She tells Cécile and me to curtsy and smile and she tells Jean to be polite and not to speak unless our father speaks to him first." Henriette took a deep breath and sucked thoughtfully on her sugar cane. Then she added, "Of course Cécile has a different father, but he doesn't live here any more."

Finally she said, "My father is white, you know, but my Oncle Félix is not. He's *gens de couleur libres*—like us."

Juliette understood and said no more. She herself was not from New Orleans, but from St. Domingue. Her father was French and her mother *gens de couleur libres*. She knew, of course, of the New Orleans custom of alliances between white men and women of color who became their mistresses. They could not marry because marriage between the races was against the law in Louisiana and throughout the Southern states. These alliances, which allowed white men to have wives and families in the white community plus colored mistresses, had been a way of life in New Orleans for many years. The free people of color were a unique and integral part of the city's population as well as an important segment of the Creole culture. Many prominent white families had relatives in the *gens de couleur libres* community.

Suddenly the girls heard a street vendor pushing a cart and loudly hawking his wares. "I got water with the melon, red to the rind!" he bellowed. "If you don't believe it, just pull up your blind! Ya eats the melon and preserves the rind!" His cries were so loud the two girls covered their ears, laughing and shaking their heads.

"I don't really like watermelon," said Juliette as they rushed past the vendor.

"I love it. It's so much fun to eat a slice and spit the seeds out as far as you can."

Juliette looked at Henriette in surprise. "You spit the seeds?"

"Sure, when we're in the patio. Not in the house, of course," Henriette laughed.

As they turned the corner onto Burgundy Street, Henriette was almost knocked down by a black boy running like crazy, his breath coming in gasps and tears running down his cheeks.

Chapter 2

The Runaway Slave

The boy stumbled, lost his balance, and fell to the ground. Juliette grabbed Henriette's arm and steadied her as they both opened their mouths to scold him. They stopped before uttering a word as they saw that the boy sprawled on the banquette was Jacques, whom they had last seen running out of the grocery with a big smile on his face.

"Jacques, what's the matter?" cried Henriette. "Why are you crying?"

Both girls reached down and helped him up. He couldn't answer at once. His breath came in fits and starts. He rubbed his eyes and sniffled, then started crying again.

"What's wrong? Are you hurt?" asked Juliette anxiously.

"It's Bevo," he finally answered in a hoarse whisper. "Dey caught him an' beat him. Ah don't know what's gonna happen to him."

"Bevo? You mean the big black man who works on the dock? Who beat him? Why did they beat him? Where is he?" asked Henriette.

Jacques wiped his nose on his shirt sleeve and sniffled some more. "He be's in da stock' by the square. I seen, 'um after I lef' your *maman's* house. His head be bleedin' an' his eyes all swol' up."

"Why, Jacques, why?"

"He dun run away. Dat man what run da dock, he work Bevo so hard, Bevo run away. He say he goin' to da bayou, to da Maroons, da swamp where he be free. But he not free, he in da stock'. He my frien'." And Jacques started to cry again.

"Oh, poor Bevo . . ." Henriette was on the verge of tears herself. She looked at Juliette, who whispered, "What can we do?"

Henriette shook her head, confused, not knowing what to say. Finally she decided. "Let's go home. Jacques, you come with us. My *maman* will give you something nice to drink and maybe a beignet. Come on, Juliette." Henriette, taking Jacques' hand, led the way, Juliette trailing behind.

At first Jacques let Henriette lead him along but he suddenly pulled away. "Ah got to go back an' see Bevo—see what ah can do to he'p him," he sobbed.

Henriette tightened her grip on his hand. They stopped in the middle of the intersection. "All right, Jacques, if you want to go see him we'll go with you," she said. Juliette sucked in her breath and held back. A carriage turned the corner and they scrambled to the banquette.

"Come on, Juliette," Henriette directed as she shepherded Jacques toward the Place d'Armes. Once on Orleans Street they saw ahead of them a cluster of men in front of the square across from Saint Louis Cathedral.

"Dat's where he be's," sobbed Jacques, pointing to the men by the square.

They walked slowly toward the square, then stopped and tried to get a glimpse of Bevo. They saw one of the men in the group clap another on the shoulder and heard him say, "I guess he won't be running away again anytime soon." They all laughed.

Now Henriette, Juliette, and Jacques could see that Bevo's hands and head were protruding from the holes in the frame of the stocks. At first, the sight reminded Henriette of a grisly puppet show. It seemed so unreal. Then she saw how swollen Bevo's face was, his eyes shut with blood oozing from one and a jagged gash above the other. A large contusion covered one side of his head, making it look lopsided. At first they thought he might be dead. Then they heard him cough, a rattling, jagged sound that seemed to come from deep inside him.

All three children gasped and moved closer. Henriette gave out a little moan and reached into her pocket, pulling out the sweet-scented handkerchief her mother had given her that morning. She started forward toward Bevo, but Juliette reached out and pulled down the hand that held the handkerchief, shaking her head back and forth.

Just then the men near the stocks turned to leave. One of them, a stout, ruddy-faced man, caught sight of the little group. "What are you girls doing here?" he shouted. "Get on home where you belong and take your sniveling slave with you." He towered over the little group, glowering and shooing them away.

The three small figures turned and retreated to the alley beside the cathedral. Henriette and Juliette began to cry and, tugging Jacques along, headed back to Henriette's house, running all the way. By the time they arrived the girls were gasping between sobs and Jacques was finally quiet, too tired and frightened to cry any more.

Henriette's mother was sitting in the living room with her needlepoint in her lap when the children burst in. "What's the matter?" she cried, seeing how upset they were. "What's happened? Look at you. You look as if you've been playing in the mud."

Henriette caught her breath after a few moments and said, "We went to see Bevo in the stocks. Oh, Maman, you should see how terrible he looks."

Pouponne dropped her needlepoint on the floor. At first it seemed she didn't know what to say. She stared at Henriette, opened and closed her mouth, then rose from her chair, a look of horror on her face, and caught her daughter by the shoulder. "You mean to tell me you went to the stocks and people saw you there? What's the matter with you? Don't you know any better? *Mon Dieu*, what am I going to do with you?"

Jacques moved back, quietly opened the door, and slipped out without being noticed.

"But Maman, we thought we could help him," Henriette started to say.

"Help him?" Pouponne interrupted. "Don't you know he ran away? He's a slave; that's what they do to runaway slaves. Respectable people don't try to help them. We are respectable, Henriette."

She turned to Juliette. "Juliette, you're older. You should know better."

Juliette dropped her eyes to the floor, started to say something, and then put a hand to her mouth and tried to stifle a sob.

"See what you've done?" Pouponne demanded as she shook Henriette. "You've upset Juliette too." She took a deep breath. "Juliette knows we're respectable people."

Pouponne turned and spoke directly to her daughter's friend. "That's all right, Juliette. We'll forget about this. But don't do any such foolish thing again, either of you. Do you hear?"

"*Oui, madame,*" they answered in unison.

Shaking her head from side to side and raising her shoulders in exasperation, she said, "We're late for dinner too. You girls go back to the kitchen and tell Nanou we're ready to eat. Call Cécile and Jean. We'll speak no more of this. And get yourselves cleaned up. You're a disgrace."

In the kitchen Henriette threw her arms around Nanou as Juliette hung back, not knowing what to do. "Come on, now, Henriette," said Nanou, "you better pay 'tention to your *maman*." But her tone was soft and loving and she gently stroked Henriette's hair.

"But what will happen to Bevo, Nanou?" Henriette asked as Nanou pulled away and turned to her pots. "I wish we could do something to help him. I think he's going to die!"

Nanou grunted. "Won't be da first time a runaway slave die. You jes have to quit worrin' so much 'bout things like dat. Nothin' you can do, dat's all. Now you both bes' go wash up, then get Jean and Cécile."

An aura of gloom hung over the meal. Henriette ate very little of the delicious gumbo Nanou served or of the fried eggplant and soft-shell crab. Cécile and Jean, aware of their mother's upset, tried to make conversation.

"Cécile, are you getting excited about your birthday party?" asked Jean.

"Weren't you excited when you turned sixteen?" she asked, trying not to look at her mother.

"As a matter of fact, I thought I was all grown up."

"That was five years ago. By now you must feel like an old man," she said with a little smile, trying to inject an air of levity into the conversation. But Jean, seeing that his mother was still scowling, just shrugged his shoulders and grinned slant-eyed at Cécile. Henriette and Juliette did not take their eyes from their plates.

When Nanou began to clear the table, Pouponne suggested that Juliette's mother might be looking for her and she had better go home. "Henriette has some needlework to finish," she added, directing a sharp glance at Henriette.

"Yes, Maman," Henriette answered softly. She knew her mother was referring to the silk shawl she was embroidering for Cécile's approaching birthday.

Soon after Juliette left, Pouponne and Cécile set off on a shopping expedition and Henriette went to her bedroom and took from the armoire the blue silk shawl she was preparing for her sister. Her mother had taught her needlework as soon as she was old enough to hold a needle and make a stitch. She loved her embroidery, partly because of earning her mother's approval, but also because it was calming.

Today as she began the stitches, she was still thinking of Bevo. "Dear Jesus," she prayed, "please help Bevo and all who suffer as he does. What can I do to help?" she asked as her needle drew in and out, following the path of her design. She finally finished the last stitch and knotted her thread. She still had no answer.

* * *

For weeks after Bevo's capture and confinement in the stocks, Henriette and Juliette prayed for him and tried to find out from Jacques what had become of him. Jacques would not speak of Bevo. His cheery manner and sunny disposition had abandoned him. He seldom smiled and was often quiet and unresponsive when he delivered groceries to Henriette's home.

Henriette asked her Uncle Félix about Bevo. He shrugged his shoulders. "A runaway slave? Who knows? Perhaps sold or sent to some plantation. We won't hear of him again around here, Henriette. You'd better forget him, put him out of your mind. He should have had better sense."

Henriette was afraid to mention Bevo again to her mother, but one day she ventured to ask something of Cécile. "I've been thinking of Bevo and wondering what's happened to him, Cécile. Where do you think he could be? Do you think he's still alive?"

"How would I know?" she answered, frowning and shaking her head. "And why should you even be thinking of a runaway slave?"

"But it's so sad . . ." Henriette's voice broke as she stifled tears.

"Oh, Henriette, you're so tenderhearted. Try to get Bevo out of your mind. That's all over with. And don't, for goodness sake, say anything to Maman about him."

"Oh, no, I wouldn't do that."

From then on Henriette noticed, as she never had before, how slaves were treated in the Quarter. She knew her Uncle Félix was kind to Jacques, who worked hard but had plenty to eat and a secure place to live. He shared an outbuilding behind the grocery with an elderly slave named Emma, who cleaned and cooked for her uncle. Henriette knew they weren't free, but she couldn't imagine that either one of them would want to run away.

And of course their own slaves, Nanou and Betsy, were like part of the family. She never thought of big, cheerful, hardworking Nanou as anyone other than a comforting and loving presence in the household who had been with the family ever since Pouponne was a little girl. Betsy was much younger and always went with Henriette to the market. Until Henriette met Juliette, Betsy was her constant playmate. But it was Nanou whose loving arms enclosed her and whose soothing words calmed her when Pouponne scolded for being late for dinner or getting her shoes and skirt muddied.

Henriette didn't know what her mother would do without Nanou, who cooked, cleaned the house, and tended the vegetable garden on the far side of the patio. Betsy, too, did her share of household duties, running errands to the market or haggling with the street vendors when she was not occupied with Henriette. She wondered if Nanou's and Betsy's lives would be any different if they weren't slaves.

One day in the kitchen, she was happily helping Nanou shell peas. They were laughing at the antics of Cécile's new kitten, which was getting tangled in a ball of twine, when Henriette got up her courage and asked, "Nanou, you're happy, aren't you, living with us I mean?"

Nanou drew herself up and frowned at Henriette. "What you sayin'? Happy. . .'Course ah'm happy. Your *maman* ain't made no complaints 'gainst me, has she?"

"Oh, no, Nanou. We all love you. I just . . . I don't know . . . I was just wondering . . ."

Nanou frowned and shook her head back and forth over the pan of peas. "Miss Henriette, ah don't know what to make of you sometime. Dis mah place and ah don't know no other place, so dat's da way it is."

Henriette leaned over and hugged Nanou. She whispered, "I love you, Nanou."

Nanou held her close for a moment, then pulled away and

got up, saying, "Ah got no more time for talk. I got to git da fire goin' and finish pluckin' dat chicken."

The next day, Henriette asked Juliette if she thought their slave Mariane was happy with them. "I think so. Yes, I'm sure she is. She never complains about anything and my mother's very fond of her. Maybe," she added after a pause, "it's just the slaves who work so hard on the waterfront that are so unhappy they run away."

The girls puzzled over this as they noticed the slaves working in the market, running errands for their masters, or unloading goods on the docks. Occasionally the slaves actually sang while working. They didn't seem unhappy. But when she passed a slave market like the one on Esplanade and saw the slaves lined up on display for sale, looking forlorn and sad, she remembered old Joseph and thought again of Bevo in the stocks. Did the slaves know that God loved them? Henriette wondered. She was sure he did, just as he loved her and Juliette.

* * *

A few days before Cécile's birthday, Henriette brought the shawl she had embroidered to show her mother while she was resting. Pouponne examined the stitches carefully, running her fingers over the tiny rose buds then turning the fabric over several times.

"Yes, Henriette, you've learned that fine embroidery must be as beautiful on the back side as on the front. Cécile will love this shawl you've made for her. It's good work."

"Merci, Maman, it was you who taught me how to do it."

"Don't you do needlework at school?"

"Not often, Maman, we do mostly reading and writing and sums. But my favorite subject is religion. Sister Ste Marthe makes the Bible stories so real."

"I see, and do you have a favorite Bible story?"

"One of my favorites is the wedding of Cana. Jesus' mother

tells him they're running out of wine, so he does his first miracle and changes water into wine."

"Well, yes, we can see that Jesus approves of wine."

"And it was also a nice gift for the married couple."

Pouponne did not respond to this last remark and Henriette sensed that her mother's silence might have some meaning. She ventured to ask, "Maman, we celebrate birthdays and baptisms in our family; why don't we have weddings to celebrate?"

The look on Pouponne's face was a combination of dismay and irritation. "Henriette, don't you realize that an alliance is a more satisfying arrangement for women like us?"

Henriette looked searchingly at her mother. "Maman, by 'women like us,' do you mean free women of color?"

"I mean octoroons, quadroons, and mulattoes. You and Cécile are octoroons; you have just one-eighth Negro blood. I am quadroon with one-fourth, and your grandmother was a mulatto: half Negro and half white. Our alliances go all the way back to your great-grandmother."

"Why didn't they just get married?"

"Henriette, you know it's against the law for mixed races to marry. Besides, most of those white men were already married to white women."

"You mean they had two wives? Does God allow that?"

"Henriette! It's not like that. But, for us, an alliance is a better arrangement. No money worries, a nice house to live in, knowing your children will be educated. God wants people to have a good life, doesn't he?"

"Yes, but what about the slaves? They don't have a good life."

"What are you saying, Henriette? Look at Nanou and Betsy. We provide everything for them. They have a wonderful life."

"I didn't mean our slaves. But slaves who run away, like Bevo. They're not happy."

"Well, that's not our fault. It depends on their owners. Can't you see that?"

"I guess so, Maman, but . . ." Her voice trailed off. Outwardly, Henriette appeared to acquiesce to her mother's reasoning but her mind was not at rest. Though she could see advantages in being provided for, she wondered if an alliance was really as good as a marriage.

Pouponne was quick to change the subject. Taking her daughter by the hand, she rose and said, "Henriette, come look at this beautiful mahogany box lined with mother of pearl. Oncle Félix found it for Cécile. Why don't we put the shawl you've embroidered here inside with Cécile's other gifts?"

"Oh, yes, Maman. What a lovely idea. She'll be so surprised; I know she's going to love it!"

"Now be off with you," Pouponne said, waving toward the door of her bedroom. "The party's in two days, and there's much to be done. Go down and help Betsy finish polishing the silver."

"Of course, Maman."

The following two days, the house was buzzing with activity in preparation for Cécile's birthday. On the day of the party, guests—Uncle Félix as well as other aunts and uncles and close friends—began arriving around 4:00 P.M. All were on hand to share the occasion. The most honored guest was Père Antoine, who brought gifts of champagne for Pouponne and a lovely medallion of the Blessed Mother for Cécile.

After everyone had finished the delicious lemon cream cake dessert, the laughter and chatter died down and Père Antoine rose to toast Cécile. But no sooner had he raised his glass than Cécile's kitten, under the table, suddenly decided to play hide-and-seek in the folds of Père Antoine's habit. The priest jumped back and began pulling on his robes with one hand while still holding his champagne glass in the other.

"What is it, what's the matter?" cried Pouponne. Several others at the table rose in alarm to rush to Père Antoine's side. But just then the kitten dashed out from under the cassock and began turning round and round on the carpet, chasing its tail. Cécile ran over and snatched it up as everyone, including Père Antoine, burst out laughing.

"You will notice that my glass is still full," he declared triumphantly, waving it back and forth. Turning to Cécile he bowed and raised his glass to her, "And may your life be full—with many blessings and much happiness."

No one wished for that more than Henriette.

Chapter 3

The Flurry of the Ball

One year later, there was again much activity in the Delille household as the fall season drew near. Cécile was more excited than ever about the coming balls and her prospects of a future alliance, prospects about which Henriette felt as ambivalent as ever. She knew that Cécile was following in her mother's footsteps and would not be married in the Church.

At school, both Henriette and Juliette were deeply influenced by Sister Ste Marthe, a member of the Dames Hospitalières, who had come to New Orleans from France in 1817 and lived with the Ursuline nuns. Since the Ursulines could accept white girls only, Sister opened a school for girls of color. Her sunny disposition and positive attitude drew students like a magnet. When she learned of the system of alliances in New Orleans, she often spoke of avoiding them in favor of the sacrament of marriage.

It was just after Cécile stopped attending school and began spending much time on her appearance that Henriette tried to talk to her sister about her misgivings concerning alliances. "Cécile," she said one day as they sat together embroidering. "I miss you so much at Sister Ste Marthe's. I wish you were still in school with us."

Cécile didn't skip a stitch as she replied with a little smile. "You know I'm not going back to school, Henriette. I'm seventeen now, and Maman says it's time for me to plan my future. School is fine for you, but when you're as old as I am you'll feel just the way I do and school won't interest you anymore."

"Oh, I'm not so sure, Cécile. I love school. I can't imagine that I would ever want to leave Sister Ste Marthe."

Cécile laughed and shook her head. Henriette looked up and realized, for the first time perhaps, how beautiful her sister was. Her ivory complexion seemed to glow, her long-lashed brown eyes sparkled, and when she held her head loftily to one side, she looked positively aristocratic. "I bet you'll be the most beautiful girl at the ball," she said.

They stitched for a time in silence. Then Henriette frowned and tried again to speak about what was on her mind. "Sister Ste Marthe doesn't like the balls. I don't think she would really want me to go to them."

"Well, you'd better not tell Maman that! You know, Henriette, not every Creole girl has the chance to go to the balls, and even the ones who do go don't all get asked to dance."

Henriette sat in silence, pondering what her sister was telling her.

"I'm sure that when it's time for your first ball you'll have a wonderful time," Cécile said, visualizing the magical atmosphere of the ballroom. "You wouldn't believe how elegant and beautiful everything is—the gowns, the music, and, of course, the dancing."

"Well, Sister Ste Marthe says . . ."

"I've heard enough about Sister. It's time for us to go down to dinner before Maman has a fit." Cécile put her embroidery on the bed and headed for the stairs.

Henriette's brow furrowed, then she slowly rose and followed her sister down to dinner.

Throughout the fall and winter, Cécile attended almost every ball of the season. Her hopes had been raised when she met a wealthy middle-aged merchant named Samuel Hart who showed great interest in her. He had asked her to dance with him on numerous occasions. One evening he spoke to Pouponne, indicating his interest in forming an alliance with

Cécile. Pouponne said she would consider his request and let him know by spring. In the meantime she planned to assure herself that he was a man of honor, someone who could be counted on to care for her daughter and any children that might issue from their alliance. Once Pouponne had ascertained his standing in the community, she shared the information with her daughters.

"He is indeed a fine gentleman. He was born in the Austrian Empire, which probably accounts for his impeccable manners. Best of all, he is an important businessman, which makes him a man of means."

As the season drew to a close, Cécile thought of just one thing: the final ball and her pending alliance. Henriette still was apprehensive about this alliance but knew she couldn't speak to her family so she confided in her best friend. "Juliette, I know it's what Maman wants for Cécile and for me too, but I really don't want to be *plaçée,* in an alliance with a white man."

"That's how I feel too," replied Juliette, who had also heard Sister Ste Marthe speak critically of the balls and the resulting alliances.

"Cécile says that I'll feel different when I'm older. But I know I never will."

Juliette smiled. "What would you like to do instead?"

"What I would really like most of all is to be like Sister Ste Marthe."

Juliette's eyes widened as she confided in turn, "So would I, Henriette. I feel exactly the same way."

Both girls respected Sister's teachings and were impressed by her deep concern for slaves. Henriette did not confide her ambition to be like Sister Ste Marthe to her mother, but she did say something to Nanou one day.

Nanou laughed and ruffled Henriette's hair. "Henriette, baby, you be's too young. Your mind might change. An' if it don't, you still got plenty time to do what you wants."

Henriette was jolted one day when she heard her mother

telling Cécile, "Henriette is about to turn twelve, and I've decided that she should go with us to the final spring ball."

Cécile was about to say something just as Henriette came into the room. "Ah, you heard that," said Pouponne. "It's important that we begin thinking of your future, my dear."

Henriette cringed, realizing that her mother was already preparing her for an eventual alliance. "But Maman, I don't think I'm ready to dance in public; I need more lessons from Mme Boileau."

"Who said anything about dancing? You're only going to observe how beautiful young ladies are expected to conduct themselves in society. Your future will depend on the impression you make at the balls."

"You're going to enjoy it, Henriette," said Cécile. "Wait till you see how much fun the balls are. And after you start dancing, you'll love it even more."

"Men will find you attractive," added Pouponne. "You know, God made you beautiful, so it must be part of his plan for you."

Henriette could think of nothing to reply and now wondered if she should even try. Obeying one's parents was also God's law and she didn't want to break a family tradition that went all the way back to her great-grandmother.

* * *

On the morning of May 21, Cécile woke early. She stretched and smiled, her head filled with thoughts of the ball that evening. Would M. Hart find her desirable? She bounded out of bed hoping that her mother would finalize arrangements for an alliance.

Cécile had an early appointment with Tatine, the *coiffeuse*. Over breakfast, Pouponne described to her daughters how adept Tatine was at her profession. "Wait till you see what she can do with just her fingers and a hairbrush. By the time she finishes with you, Cécile, you'll look and feel like a queen. You will too, Henriette, when your turn comes."

Henriette did not respond. For the moment, she was glad she didn't have to spend all morning having someone fuss with her hair.

Cécile looked wistfully at her mother and asked, "Do you think M. Hart will find me beautiful?"

"My dear, he will not only find you beautiful, he will be proud to claim you. And now that I know of his background, I've decided to finalize plans for your alliance."

Cécile gave a sharp cry of delight, "Oh, Maman, this is the most exciting day of my whole life."

Henriette stood wide-eyed and silent. Somewhere inside herself she thought she heard a heavy door slam shut.

"Now girls, I hope you understand that this is a very serious decision. Cécile, it means you are giving your life to this man. You'll bear his children and be responsible for raising them."

"Maman, do you think he'll send our children to France to be educated as some men do?"

"I doubt he would since he's not French, but he'll provide for their education and everything they need."

Henriette dared to ask her mother, "Maman, since M. Hart is a bachelor, do you think Père Antoine could bless this alliance?"

Visibly annoyed, Pouponne looked sternly at her daughter. "Henriette, you know the answer to that question. These partnerships started here in the 1700s; it's our way of life. Furthermore, Père Antoine has never said a word against them."

"Father Portier says that's because he doesn't want to anger the people who contribute to the cathedral," ventured Henriette.

"Did he now? Well, we all know Father Portier is young, and he's not from here. He doesn't understand our customs."

Henriette thought it best not to mention that Father Portier had made it quite clear that such arrangements were immoral and ought to be discouraged.

"Enough gloomy talk, girls. Go about your business now and be back here for dinner. We need the afternoon to get ready for the ball."

Henriette wasn't thinking of the ball as she got ready for school. Instead, she was regretting that because this date had fallen on a Thursday, she would miss teaching the slave children who came for Bible story classes in the afternoon. She thought of how their eyes glowed at Christmastime when she explained that baby Jesus was born in a stable and that angels sang in the sky and told shepherds to go see him. She also told them how Jesus grew up poor and spent his life curing sick people. During Lent, she spoke of his suffering and death on the cross and how he forgave everyone, even the people who put him to death. The children listened spellbound when she told them God loved them more than they could imagine and that he always heard their prayers. At such times, Henriette felt she would like nothing better than to spend her whole life working with these children. Of course, Pouponne would be outraged if she thought Henriette harbored such ideas.

After morning classes, as Henriette was heading home for dinner, she nearly collided with her sister rounding the corner out of breath. "Cécile, what's wrong?" she asked.

"Wrong? Nothing's wrong," she answered. "Maman was right, Tatine certainly is an artist! Just look at how she's woven tiny seed pearls into my hair," she said turning her head from side to side for Henriette to admire.

"It's lovely, but did it really take all morning? How could you sit still so long?"

"I didn't mind a bit. Henriette, aren't you excited about tonight? Your first ball?"

"Not as excited as you must be. I'm very curious to meet your M. Hart."

"Don't worry, you'll meet him. He's ever so nice and quite handsome too!"

"Tell me, Cécile. Do you love him?" asked Henriette, looking very serious.

"Yes . . . Well, I think I do. Maman says since he's well-mannered and rich, it's sure to be a good match." Henriette wondered if a good match was the same as love.

As the girls entered the front door Pouponne called to them, "Cécile, Henriette, I'm glad you're back. The dressmaker has laid your ball gowns up in my room."

"Wonderful!" squealed Cécile. "When can we start to get ready?"

"First, let's have dinner. Then we should rest so we'll be fresh for the evening."

After the noon meal, Henriette and Cécile followed their mother upstairs where on the bed lay two beautiful white dresses, one in satin, the other in crisp tulle.

"Oh, satin, how beautiful," chirped Cécile breathlessly.

"I love mine too, Maman. You always know what looks good," agreed Henriette.

After the girls took a refreshing nap, Nanou prepared lavender-scented bathwater for each of them. They donned handmade undergarments of fine white batiste along with white lace stockings. Both girls felt very grown up as they slid their feet into satin pumps. Cécile then donned numerous petticoats, which would cause her satin dress to sway gracefully with each step she took.

"Now, Cécile, sit on this stool so I can help you with your dress," commanded Pouponne. When she had finished fastening the tiny buttons down the back she sighed, "There now, get up and slowly walk to the mirror."

Cécile rose and floated across the room. At the sight of her reflection in the cheval mirror, she caught her breath. "It's so beautiful!" she gasped. "Maman, I simply love it."

"Wait, Cécile, we're not finished yet," laughed Pouponne. She took from her jewelry box a diamond pendant which she securely fastened around her daughter's neck. "This was given to me long ago by your father. He is no longer with us, but this is a lovely keepsake. I'm sure he'd want you to have it."

Both girls drew in their breath. "Maman," whispered Cécile, "it's much too fine."

Pouponne and Henriette stood back and gazed admiringly at Cécile.

"Cécile, you look so grown up," remarked Henriette.

"She is grown up," said her mother and gazed at her elder daughter. "My darling, M. Hart will be proud to stroll through the ballroom with you on his arm."

Henriette, too, thought her sister looked beautiful, yet she was uneasy. Once the alliance was finalized, Cécile would belong to this man. She tried to remain cheerful, but her serious expression and her silence caused Pouponne to inquire, "Henriette, you're very quiet. Don't you know this is an important night for Cécile?"

"Yes, Maman . . ." She hesitated and then blurted out, "but it can never be a real marriage!"

Pouponne frowned at her daughter. "Listen, Henriette. You need to understand that this match is right for Cécile. She is following our family tradition. Not even if she married a free man of color would she be so well taken care of."

"But, Maman . . ."

Pouponne threw up her hands in exasperation, shook her head, and scolded, "Don't you think your sister would love to be dressed as a bride and have a big wedding at the cathedral?"

At this, Cécile came close to tears. "It's not my fault that a white man can't marry me," she wailed.

"Of course not, my darling," interjected Pouponne, putting an arm around Cécile's shoulder. "We've always been respectable people and have lived good lives. All of us have had white fathers for generations, all the way back to great Grand-Maman. That's just the way it was—and still is. And it will be for you too, Henriette, when the time comes."

"Maman, I don't want an arrangement. I want to stay free so I can . . ."

"What kind of talk is that?" her mother shrieked. "We are

free, Henriette! We're free people of color and always will be in spite of whatever ridiculous ideas that nun has put into your head." Pouponne was now shouting and close to hysteria. "Now finish dressing and don't bring this up again. If you're trying to ruin our whole evening, you're doing a good job."

When Pouponne stopped shouting the silence in the room was palpable. Both girls looked at their mother, who was breathing heavily. Then, in an effort to regain a sense of normalcy, Cécile caught her breath and murmured, "Maman, do you think we could go out to the balcony and find a nice flower for your hair? That big urn has some gardenias blooming."

Pouponne looked confused and seemed to have lost her focus. "Yes . . . " she finally said, then whispered, "That's a good idea."

As the two of them left the room, Henriette sank down on her mother's bed and drew a deep breath. She was sorry to have caused so much discord, especially since she knew her mother wanted a good life for her children. Yet, in spite of it, something inside Henriette, in her heart of hearts, resisted. She simply did not want to go against the teachings of her Catholic faith. Bowing her head she prayed, "Dear Lord, please show me what you want me to do." She took a deep breath and tried to relax. Closing her eyes, she envisioned the Lord as he changed water into wine at the wedding feast at Cana. Slowly, her breathing slowed and peace returned to her spirit.

When Cécile came back into the room Henriette was still seated on the bed, smiling slightly and apparently lost in thought. "Hurry, Henriette, get dressed. It's almost time to leave and we don't want Maman to be upset again."

Henriette's eyes widened as she looked at her sister. "Oh, I'll be ready in a few minutes." She quickly stepped into her dress and let Cécile button her up. Pouponne came into the room and seemed to glow with anticipation. Henriette was surprised at how much her mother's mood had changed in such a short time.

"Oh, Maman, you look beautiful," she said, "as if you could be Cécile's sister."

"Nonsense," replied Pouponne, smiling at the flattery. "Anyone can see I'm much older," she said and calmly fastened a string of pearls around Henriette's neck. "Now put on your white gloves and tuck a lace handkerchief into your evening bag. And for a final touch, a bit of perfume for both of you."

The three of them descended the stairs, bringing with them the faint scent of honeysuckle. Nanou was waiting for them in the foyer. "Oh, Ma'am Pouponne, jes look at you . . . so purty! An jes look at ma li'l babies. They's all growed up."

"Yes, they are," said Pouponne. "Don't wait up for us, Nanou. We probably won't get home till very late. Not till the wee hours."

"No ma'am. I sure be sleepin' then. Y'all have a good time. And Miss Cécile, you be's purty nuff to catch any man you wants." At that, the house rang with laughter.

When they opened the front door, Jacques was there with his lantern, waiting to escort the three of them through the dark city streets. Approaching the large portals of the Quadroon Ballroom, they heard the night air ring with greetings. *"Bonsoir,* Mathilde." *"Bonsoir, Amélie!"* *"Quelle jolie robe!"* Henriette had never seen such a bevy of gorgeous gowns, flowing boas, and nodding plumes all making their way through the open portals. As they ascended the grand staircase, Henriette's eyes grew wide with wonder.

When she entered the ballroom, ablaze with candles burning in crystal chandeliers, she couldn't help muttering in amazement, "Why, it's simply gorgeous."

"Didn't I tell you?" whispered Cécile.

Henriette breathed in the sweet aroma of spring flowers. She let her eyes sweep through the hall, glancing at the giant bouquets of magnolias placed near the walls, white-gloved waiters with silver trays, and in the center a large serving table with punch bowls and delicious delicacies. Elegantly attired mothers and daughters were scurrying about the room laughing and chattering as they looked for empty tables. Henriette smiled and stood erect as her mother had instructed but couldn't quite bring herself to toss her head, delicately finger her pearls, or flash her eyes as so many young ladies were doing. Her mother and sister seemed totally at ease in this setting. She, on the other hand, though dazzled, felt out of place. It was against her nature to want to draw attention to herself in this way.

"Over here, girls," called Pouponne, claiming one of the tables near an open window.

Cécile took hold of Henriette, who was still watching the fairytale scene unfold before her. A small orchestra began tuning at the far end of the room. As the room filled and the music began, ladies and gentlemen were enjoying each other's company. Some were dancing, others visiting, chatting, enjoying a glass of champagne, and obviously having a wonderful time. Henriette was beginning to understand why a young girl surrounded by the excitement of such thrilling sights and sounds might give in to romantic fantasies.

Shortly after they had been seated and were sipping their first punch of the evening, M. Hart, a handsome sight in white tie and tails, came over to Pouponne's table. *"Bonsoir, madame.* May I presume that this is your other daughter?" he asked Pouponne.

"Yes, *monsieur,* this is Henriette, my youngest child."

Taking hold of Henriette's hand and bowing from the waist, he greeted her. Henriette smiled and responded with a gracious nod of her head, thinking to herself how old he looked. Just then the orchestra began playing and M. Hart turned to Cécile, offering her his arm, "My dear Cécile, may I have the honor?"

Cécile flushed. *"Oui, monsieur, avec plaisir."* And he escorted her to the middle of the dance floor.

Pouponne and Henriette settled themselves to watch the dancers swirl to the sounds of a lilting waltz. Noting her sister's happy expression, Henriette could see that Cécile was content to carry on the family tradition. She was still watching the dancers when a handsome young man approached the table and greeted them. "*Bonsoir, madame. Bonsoir, mademoiselle.*" Turning to Henriette he said, "May I have the honor of the next dance, *mademoiselle?*" Henriette stiffened. She turned to Pouponne, uncertain of how to respond.

"*Oh, non, monsieur,*" her mother quickly intervened. "My daughter is too young. This is her first ball and she is here just to observe." The young man's expression changed to one of disappointment. He bowed graciously and backed away, saying, "Ah, what a shame; she is so beautiful. Another time perhaps."

Henriette, clasping her mother's arm and breathing a sigh of relief, whispered, "*Merci,* Maman. I didn't know how to refuse him politely." She thought it best not to explain that all her negative feelings about alliances had returned in an instant. In no way did she wish to encourage a relationship that might lead to her own commitment. Why take even one step in a direction she was not willing to pursue?

The evening passed quickly with much visiting back and forth among the tables, dancing, promenading, and dining, all with much laughter and gaiety. Pouponne and M. Hart arranged to meet on the *levée* the next afternoon to sign the terms of the alliance with Cécile, which would include a large two-story house on Orleans Avenue and a monthly stipend for her expenses. Because the house was very large, M. Hart suggested to Pouponne that she and her household would be welcome to move into the residence with Cécile.

When Henriette heard that Cécile's future had been secured, scenes of the ball flashed through her mind. It seemed strange that such a frivolous occasion could lead to such a momentous and serious undertaking. In her musing she wondered if God might be using this same frivolous occasion to draw her to himself. "Dear Lord," she whispered, "could it be that you're asking me to form an alliance with you?" She smiled.

Chapter 4

Sister Ste Marthe's Influence

The day after the ball, Pouponne and her daughters slept late, but by eleven o'clock they were up and sitting in the patio discussing the events of the previous evening. Nanou served *café au lait* and beignets, listening all the while to hear the highlights of the ball. She was delighted that M. Hart had asked for an alliance with Cécile, which, after all, everyone had been expecting, but she could hardly believe it when she heard that they would all be moving with Cécile to a lovely house on Orleans Avenue.

"Maman, I'm so glad we can stay together as a family," said Cécile. "It'll be wonderful having you and Henriette with me." As she was speaking she saw Nanou's eyes grow large with astonishment, so added, "And Nanou, you and Betsy will be coming too."

"What do you think of that, Nanou?" asked Henriette.

"Ain't ma place to say," said Nanou, "but ah never heard anybody *placer* da whole family." At this they all laughed heartily.

"Well, it is unusual, Nanou, but since M. Hart is single and very rich, he offered to let us stay together. I think that speaks very well of him," Pouponne declared.

"Yes, ma'am, it do."

"He's certainly generous," agreed Henriette.

"Now that Jean has his own place and is working in real estate," said Pouponne, "I think I'll ask him to put this house up for rent. We don't need two houses and extra income is always welcome."

"When do you think we'll be able to move, Maman? Should we start packing?" asked Cécile.

"When I meet M. Hart this afternoon, we'll work out the details of this alliance. We need to find out the condition of the house. I'm sure he plans to have it ready quite soon."

Within a few weeks, Cécile was settled in her new abode. The rest of the household soon followed and before long everyone was comfortable in their new home. Pouponne, especially, enjoyed the new location in the French Quarter. It was closer to the cathedral and to the Place d'Armes, the very center of activity in the Quarter.

As time passed, Henriette attended other balls with her mother, but her ambivalence about alliances remained strong. Now age thirteen, her primary focus was at the St. Claude School, which was flourishing with an enrollment of eighty free girls of color. Henriette and Juliette noticed that it was more work than Sister Ste Marthe could manage and that she depended increasingly on them and their new friend, Joséphine Charles, for help.

One Thursday afternoon in March, as classes were breaking up, Sister stopped the three of them. "Girls, the nine-year-olds will be making their First Holy Communion this spring. Can you help me teach them their prayers?" she asked, looking very tired.

"Oh yes, Sister," the girls responded in unison.

"When would you like us to start?" asked Joséphine.

"Next week, if it's not too much to ask."

"I have to help my mother after school," said Joséphine. "She depends on me to take care of my brothers and sisters. But I'll ask her if I can help you next week and let you know tomorrow morning."

"That will be just fine, Joséphine. You run along now and I'll see you tomorrow."

With that, Joséphine bade them all good-bye and left for home.

"Sister, I can help you," offered Henriette. "I love teaching the children."

"And so do I," added Juliette.

"I know you do, and the children love you. Our dear Lord must surely be pleased," replied the nun, "but I want you girls to pray very hard. Since we opened back in 1823 the school has grown, but it's now in a lot of trouble." She confided, "We need money badly and we also need more teachers."

While Sister Ste Marthe was speaking to the girls, she was interrupted by the sound of someone running into the building. When they looked up, Father Portier appeared in the doorway to say that Emmeline, one of the slaves belonging to the Beauchamp family, was about to give birth but that things were not going well.

"Sister, please come quickly," he said. "Emmeline has been struggling for hours in labor. By now the baby must be born. We need to pray for Emmeline and baptize the baby right away. Girls, come along with Sister."

They rushed several blocks from the school to the three-story townhouse on the corner of Royal and Dumaine Streets. Out of breath, they scurried through the alleyway leading to the slave quarters behind the courtyard. At the entrance to the narrow dwelling, high-pitched baby cries reached their ears and an acrid smell tweaked their nostrils.

When they entered the semi-darkened room, they saw two slaves, one on each side of the bed, holding onto Emmeline as she gasped for breath. They moaned soft words of encouragement, trying to get her to relax. A third slave sat in the corner cuddling a whimpering bundle in her arms.

Sister Ste Marthe joined the two women next to the bed. Henriette and Juliette simply stared at the scene before them while Father Portier stood in the doorway. Several minutes passed. They listened as Emmeline's breathing became shallow and halting. They heard a deep sigh. Everyone waited for the next sound, but it never came. Emmeline lay very still, her eyes closed, her face expressionless. Silence engulfed the room. Even the baby was quiet.

Then, "She done passed," sobbed Lulie, one of the slaves who had been assisting the laboring woman. "Emmeline done passed."

"Oh, no," said Father, visibly shocked, and rushed to the bedside.

"She been strugglin' so hard, and she be hurtin' bad," said Lulie, shaking her head.

"We done what we could to he'p her . . . but she was too weak and worn out," said the other slave, Dina, through her tears.

Henriette and Juliette couldn't believe what had happened. Their young friend was lying lifeless on a bed of crumpled sheets drenched with blood and perspiration. That someone so close to their own age could die was incomprehensible. They had first met Emmeline when she came to Sister Ste Marthe's school for catechism. After that, they had seen her almost daily in the Quarter or in the French Market buying things for Mme Beauchamp.

"I talked to Emmeline a few days ago," whispered Juliette. "She told me her baby was due any day but she looked fine."

"I saw her in church," added Henriette, choking back her tears. "She was so happy waiting for her baby."

"Her baby be's awright," said a muffled voice from the corner, and Beulah got up to show them the tiny child. "It be's a li'l boy," she said. "Seems like when Emmeline knowed he gwine be awright she jes gave up."

Father Portier looked up and said, "First we'll say the prayers for the dying, and then we'll baptize the baby." Beulah returned to the corner, weeping softly as she sat swaying back and forth cuddling her bundle. Father took his breviary from the pocket of his habit. All knelt as he recited the Nunc Dimittis and the De Profundis.

Still kneeling, Henriette, her hands covering her tears, felt someone touch her shoulder. "Will you be the baby's baptismal sponsor?" asked Father. Without answering she leapt to her feet and retrieved the baby from Beulah's arms. Peering down at the tiny face, she gathered new courage.

"We need some water. Is there any here in the room?" asked the priest.

"Yes, Father. Here be's some," said Lulie, taking the granite pitcher from the nightstand.

"Good. Now what name shall we give this child?" he asked, looking around.

"Benjamin," said Dina. "Emmeline said she wanna name him Benjie jes like his papa."

"That's a fine name," he answered and began the rite of baptism.

As the baby's sponsor, Henriette, her voice now strong, renounced Satan and all his works. Sister Ste Marthe led the others in the responses and in the Apostle's Creed.

As soon as Father finished pouring the water and pronouncing the words, "I baptize thee, Benjamin, in the Name of the Father, and of the Son, and of the Holy Spirit," the baby began to cry.

"He be's hungry," said Beulah, "I gwine get 'im some milk." And she left the room.

"We need to find him a wet nurse, Lulie," said Sister Ste Marthe. "Are there any nursing mothers nearby?"

"Yes ma'am, I knows a slave be nursin' her baby; she live in St. Louis Street. She be glad to he'p Emmeline's baby," offered Lulie. "You want me to fetch Annie Mae?"

"Yes, go see when she can come, Lulie. We'll have to inform the Beauchamps of what has happened. Mme Beauchamp needs to see about someone to care for this child."

Beulah returned shortly with a knotted towel soaked in sugar and warm milk. The baby, now back in her arms, stopped crying as soon as she put the sugar-tit into his mouth.

"Now we must prepare for Emmeline's burial," said Father Portier. "I'll inform Mme Beauchamp on my way out and see when she wants the funeral to take place. Then I'll go to the rectory and make the arrangements. Juliette, you come with me. Henriette, you'd best stay here and help Sister Ste Marthe and Dina prepare the body."

Some time later Juliette returned to say that the funeral was scheduled for the next morning at the Mortuary Chapel. In the meantime, Emmeline's body had been washed and freshly clothed and was lying peacefully in state. The bed, now fresh and clean, had been pulled to the center of the room with a lighted candle on either side. News of Emmeline's death was already spreading throughout the Quarter. Mme Beauchamp, followed by some of the household slaves, arrived to pay their respects. Many more would come throughout the night, for Emmeline was loved and would be sorely missed.

Henriette was concerned about little Benjamin. She turned to Sister Ste Marthe and beckoned her out to the courtyard. "How can this baby grow up without his mother? What will happen to him?"

"Legally he belongs here with the Beauchamp family," Sister answered.

"But they won't love little Benjie as a mother would. Couldn't he be with his father?"

"Unfortunately he was sold several months ago. He can't do anything for the child."

A wave of anger swept over Henriette as she realized again the evil impact of slavery. Who or what gave one man the right to own another human being? Why couldn't a father claim his own son? How could people be so insensitive to human suffering?

Nothing would have pleased Henriette more than to take Benjie home and care for him herself. She remembered other times when she was unable to change a heartbreaking situation. Scenes of Bevo suffering in the stocks and old Joseph sold on the block passed through her mind. And now, as she thought of Benjie growing up without parents, her helplessness and frustration returned. "Dear Lord," she brooded, "this is so unfair! Someone must do something."

Henriette slept fitfully the next two nights, deeply disturbed by the questions surrounding Emmeline's death. The morning after the funeral, she went to the rectory to speak with Father Portier.

"Father, do you remember my telling you that I don't wish to form an alliance with a white man like my sister, Cécile, did?"

"Of course, Henriette, I remember very well," he said, sensing her serious mood. "I pray that more young women like you and Juliette will renounce alliances and choose to marry in the Church and raise solid families. It's the only way to stop this immoral custom that's against God's law."

"But Father, I don't wish to marry either," she responded. "I want to do something to help the slaves. I want to be like Sister Ste Marthe."

"It seems to me you've already started," he said with a little smile. "And when you finish your schooling, I'm sure Sister would welcome you as a full-time teacher."

"Yes, Father. But what I mean is," she paused, then said, "I want to be a nun. That way I can spend my whole life helping slaves."

Father Portier's smile broadened as he said, "Oh, Henriette, you're still very young. How old are you now? Thirteen? Fourteen?"

"I'll soon be fourteen, Father."

"Very well, but before you consider such a step you must be sure that God is truly calling you. The vocation of a vowed religious is not for everyone."

"What do you mean, Father? Is it because I come from *gens de couleur?*"

"No, that's not the problem. Many religious orders in France would gladly accept a person of color. What I mean is that the life of a religious is disciplined and very demanding. Not every individual has the background and temperament to commit to it."

Henriette was stunned. Instead of offering words of encouragement as she had expected, Father Portier seemed to be discouraging her. Was he implying that because of her privileged background she was unfit for a life of sacrifice?

"But Father, I see how hard Sister Ste Marthe works every day. I'm sure I could do what she does. And she needs help badly."

"Then continue helping her as you have been. In the meantime, look around you. There are many fine, hardworking young men of color who would make excellent husbands. In a year or two you may meet someone and fall in love."

"But Father, right now I'm thinking of little Benjie, born

a slave," she said. "He has no mother or father to raise him. What's to become of him?"

"I know slavery is a cruel system, Henriette, but not even Sister Ste Marthe can do anything about Benjamin." He stood and reached for his notebook.

"I have an appointment now to see the bishop. You need to pray for God's guidance. If it's truly his will for you to pursue this idea, he'll show you the way." He escorted her to the door of the rectory, bade her good-bye, and waved her on her way.

Henriette trudged toward home, her heart as heavy as the leaden skies over the French Quarter. She hardly noticed the light rain falling. Not wanting to face her family in her present state of sadness and confusion, she continued past her house toward Rampart Street and the Mortuary Chapel. Flowers from Emmeline's funeral were still in the sanctuary when she slipped into the little church, dark now except for the light from the sanctuary lamp. Tears ran down her cheeks as she tried to pray, but no words would come. Her tangled thoughts revolved around baby Benjamin and Father Portier's discouraging advice about her future.

Finally she prayed, "Dear Lord, I know that being a wife and mother would be wonderful, but I don't think it's for me. If I could live as Sister Ste Marthe does, I would spend all my time working with the slaves. That's what I desire more than anything. Isn't that the message you've been giving me? It's hard enough trying to convince my mother and sister of that. Must I now convince Father Portier too?"

She sat back into the bench as if expecting a reply. Outside the chapel the rain was now pouring relentlessly. She took a deep breath, closed her eyes, and whispered resolutely, "Lord, I'm not leaving till you tell me what I'm supposed to do."

A long time passed. She thought of Sister Ste Marthe and the Ursuline nuns. How she wished she could join their ranks and give her life to God. Could Father Portier be right? Should she consider going to France and joining a religious order there? She knew of many black Creole families who sent their sons to France to be educated and to learn a profession. Many of them never returned.

Tears burned her eyes as she considered such a prospect. "Besides, dear Lord," she prayed, "You know there are no slaves in France. Here in New Orleans is where they are and they need help."

She waited. Gradually the rain stopped, the chapel grew completely silent. High above the altar she saw the reflection of the glowing sanctuary lamp. The gentle flicker had a soothing effect on her and she felt her body relax. She continued to sit quietly until she felt herself surrounded by the warmth of sunlight, now streaming through the windows. With it, her inner peace returned and Henriette knew she had her answer. The sky may darken and the rain may fall, but the sun doesn't stop shining. It has merely gone behind the clouds and in time it will return.

She slipped to her knees and, looking at the tabernacle, whispered, "Thank you, Lord. You've given me my answer. I know that one day you'll show me how to help the slaves."

The next afternoon Henriette met Father Portier on Chartres Street coming from the direction of the cathedral. "Good afternoon, Father," she said smiling.

"Hello, Henriette. Have you considered the advice I gave you yesterday?" he asked.

"Oh yes, Father. I'm praying for God's guidance, just as you said."

"Good girl. And Henriette, please pray for me. I'll be leaving New Orleans shortly on a new assignment."

"Leaving New Orleans? Oh, Father, you don't have to go back to France, do you?

"No, Henriette," he replied, "not so far. Just to Mobile. I've been appointed vicar apostolic, overseeing Alabama and Florida, so I'll be traveling quite a bit. We never know where God will lead us, do we?"

"No, Father," she answered, feeling a tingle of recognition. "But we'll miss you here."

"I'll need your prayers, Henriette."

"Of course, Father, I'll pray for you every day," she answered smiling. Then, waving good-bye, she turned and continued on her way.

Chapter 5

In Society

Within a year of her alliance, Cécile had given birth to a beautiful baby girl. Though M. Hart was Jewish, he had no objection to having the child baptized in the Catholic Church. On the appointed Sunday afternoon, family and friends gathered at the baptismal font in St. Louis Cathedral. Père Antoine was there to officiate at Pouponne's request.

"And what name are we going to give this baby?" asked the priest.

"We'd like to call her Antoinette, Père, after you," said Cécile, smiling at their beloved pastor.

Père Antoine chuckled aloud and said, "Oh ho! What an excellent choice."

Then, looking fondly at the infant, "All right, little Antoinette, let's make a Christian out of you and snatch you away from the snares of Satan."

The baby cooed throughout the ceremony. Henriette, who had sponsored many children among the slave population, was proud to be the godmother of her own niece, bedecked in a long white christening gown. And there by her side, her brother, Jean, now married and living in St. Martinville, was back in town to become the proud godfather.

After the church ceremony, the guests poured into the patio of Cécile's home on Orleans Street. Nanou and Betsy, both dressed in their Sunday best and each wearing a gleaming white apron, passed in and out among the guests with trays of dainty sandwiches and assorted sweets. M. Hart had sent his slave, Jefferson, with several bottles of the finest French champagne.

The baby, now cradled in Jean's arms, was the center of attention as Père Antoine raised his glass in a toast to the newly baptized infant. "To my new namesake. I wish little Antoinette a long and happy life, filled with all good things on God's green earth."

The years of Cécile's alliance with M. Hart flew by. As a woman in *plaçage* she no longer attended the balls which had previously given her so much pleasure, but the joys of motherhood seemed to satisfy her well enough so that she no longer missed them. On the other hand, Pouponne still required Henriette to attend them, but frequent headaches and bouts of melancholy prevented her *maman* from leaving the house. At those times Henriette would either skip the balls or go with friends. She would have liked to go with Juliette and Joséphine but they seldom went to the balls as their parents expected them to marry—especially Joséphine, who at sixteen already had several suitors asking for her hand.

Living in the same house with her sister gave Henriette a chance to observe the kind of relationship Cécile enjoyed with M. Hart. She had the distinct impression that if she and her mother were not sharing the house with her, Cécile would be very lonely, in spite of her motherhood. After the alliance, M. Hart came to dinner and to visit at least once or twice a week, but gradually his visits became less frequent even though he lived nearby. Often he was out of the country for weeks at a time.

As for Henriette herself, she was caught between working with Sister Ste Marthe at school and helping Cécile with Antoinette at home, where she enjoyed interludes of family fun. One such occasion was an afternoon in mid-March. Sun streamed into the colorful courtyard, intensifying the brilliant bloom of azalea bushes and the sweet fragrance of white jasmine. Pouponne, sitting in the shade of the banana trees, cooled herself with a palmetto fan. She had been ailing and had recently kept to her room, but today she was content to sit and watch her grandchild enjoy a game of "keep away." Antoinette, now a toddler at age three, had been scuttling back and forth between Cécile and Henriette for the last half-hour, offering her rag doll first to one and then the other.

"Oh, thank you, Antoinette," Henriette beamed, holding out her hands. But before her *tante* could take hold of it, Antoinette snatched the doll from her grasp and ran, squealing with delight, back to her mother. The instant she got within arm's reach, Cécile scooped up baby and doll together, hugging them tightly in her arms.

"I think someone's going to wear herself out if she doesn't stop now and have a nap," laughed Cécile. Antoinette tossed her head back and forth as she struggled and squirmed but Cécile held her fast. As she carried her daughter up the stairs they all heard a loud knock at the door.

Nanou called from the kitchen, "Miss Henriette, can you answer the door? I gots to stir mah roux so she don't burn. Else y'all won't be havin' *gumbo z'herbes* for supper."

"Yes, I'll get it," Henriette said as she passed through the house to the foyer. When she opened the door, M. Hart's slave, Jefferson, stood holding a large white envelope. "Hello, Jefferson. What's this?" she asked, tilting her head.

The little boy grinned at Henriette. "It's a invite for y'all from M. Hart," he said, holding it out to her. "I b'lieve it be's for the big opera."

"How kind of him," said Henriette, taking the envelope. "Please thank M. Hart and tell him we'll send our reply very soon."

"Who is it, Henriette?" called Pouponne from the patio.

"Jefferson just brought this from M. Hart," she said, handing her mother the envelope. "He says it's an invitation for us to attend the opera."

Pouponne, who had been reclusive for some time, revived quickly as she tore the seal and read aloud: "M. Hart cordially invites Cécile Bonille, Marie Joseph Diaz, and Henriette

Delille to be his guests at the Théâtre d'Orléans on Friday, March 29, 1827, at 7:00 P.M. for the return production of '*La Dame Blanche*' by M. François Boieldieu."

"Why, this is the best news we've had in a long time," she cried. "What will we wear? We must start thinking about it. It's such a special occasion and just a few weeks away. That will never be enough time for Mme Olivier to make three new outfits."

Cécile, coming down the balcony stairs, had heard her mother read the invitation as well as her comments. "But Maman, do we really need new outfits? We still have several ball gowns."

"They won't do for the opera," responded Pouponne, shaking her head. "We need elegant evening clothes, not frilly ball gowns."

Pouponne was all astir as she began planning everyone's wardrobe. "Cécile, you can wear your moss green faille dress and we'll get Mme Olivier to make you a soft paisley vest with a velvet collar. Of course you'll need a hat, new shoes, and perhaps we can find a little velvet purse to match."

Henriette, hoping to avoid being stuck with pins at another of Mme Olivier's fittings, said, "Maman, I'll wear my black velvet skirt and the white silk blouse with pearl buttons."

"Well, Henriette, that's only half an outfit. You'll need an evening jacket and of course matching accessories. Now that I think of it, Mme Olivier has some new bolts of cloth from Paris. I remember seeing a black and burgundy challis with a floral pattern. That will set off your skirt nicely."

"And what will you wear, Maman?" asked Cécile, beginning to feel the excitement that Pouponne generated for the coming event.

Pouponne's eyes were sparkling as she described her new outfit. "Well, it so happens that Mme Olivier received a number of patterns of the latest Paris fashions. She showed me an elegant peacock blue suit with a tight jacket set off by a creamy lace jabot. It was so stunning that I immediately commissioned Mme Olivier to make one for me." Then, with a tilt of her head, "Oh, and girls, there is also the most precious little opera hat—like a man's top hat but not so tall—with a veil that drops down over the face. *C'est charmant!*"

"Oh, Maman, did you know we'd be invited to the opera?" asked Cécile.

"Not at all. I was planning to wear the suit for Easter, but it will be perfect for this occasion," said Pouponne as she thought of the dashing figure she would cut.

The following weeks, Pouponne, greatly invigorated by the coming event, looked for articles about the opera in the *Courrier,* which she required the girls to read aloud after dinner. When Henriette learned that Juliette and Joséphine would be attending the same performance, she invited them to come and share in the reading sessions.

One of the articles gave such a glowing account that Pouponne exclaimed, "I've been attending the opera all my life, but this one sounds simply spectacular."

"Well, it must be very special because they've already had five performances in February and now it's back by popular demand," said Joséphine.

They continued chattering about this highlight of the season until Pouponne, looking somewhat ashen, announced, "Excuse me, girls, I have to go upstairs and rest. I'm frankly quite exhausted."

Henriette and her friends spent the rest of the afternoon playing several hands of whist, drinking China tea, and munching on tea cakes.

The night of the opera performance M. Hart himself came to escort his guests to the Théâtre d'Orléans. "Good evening, ladies," he smiled. "Don't you all look stunning." He nodded approvingly. "It's such a beautiful evening. We'll enjoy walking to the theatre. And Jefferson is here to lead us with his lantern."

Upon arrival at the opera house, M. Hart tipped an usher to escort the ladies to a center box in the second gallery, reserved for free people of color. He himself sat in the orchestra section reserved for white audience members, while Jefferson, who had also been given a ticket, climbed to the third gallery, which was reserved for slaves.

"These seats are perfect," said Henriette, delighted that they would be able to see the stage easily. "How thoughtful of M. Hart to get such fine seats."

As they settled themselves and began looking around at the audience, Henriette spied Juliette and Joséphine in the second gallery and several slaves she knew in the third. She smiled and was about to wave to them when she felt her mother's strong grip and heard her whisper sharply, "Don't you dare wave to those slaves, Henriette. In fact don't wave at all. You don't see any of those ladies in the parquet waving, do you? By now you're old enough to know how to behave properly in public."

Heeding her mother's admonition, she nevertheless continued to smile and nod her head ever so slightly to slaves in the top tier. Rather than feel chastised, Henriette chafed at "propriety" that prevented her from showing what she considered common courtesy to her acquaintances. The more she thought about it, the more she took exception to social customs that prevented acts of friendliness to one's fellow human beings.

As she pondered these thoughts, Henriette spied a familiar figure. "Look, Maman. There's Oncle Félix and he's headed right this way."

Indeed it was he, elegantly dressed in his finest evening clothes and looking very different from his usual self while minding the store. *"Bonsoir, mes chères dames, "* said Uncle Félix, bowing ceremoniously to the three of them. "What fine seats you have here." He settled himself next to Pouponne.

"They're wonderful," she answered for all of them, "and I'm glad to see that you were able to join us, Félix. But I thought you'd already seen this opera when it first opened."

"I have seen it, but it's so good I wanted to see it again. You know, this opera opened two years ago in Paris at the Opéra

Comique. The cast here is different, but we always have fine productions and this one is outstanding."

"We've read that the story is spellbinding," broke in Cécile. "Would you tell it to us before the curtain goes up?"

"I don't want to give away the surprise ending, so I'll just say that it takes place in Scotland in a haunted castle. A strange woman wearing a white dress appears regularly. She's believed to be the ghost of the castle and to possess its secret."

"So the ghost must be *la dame blanche!*" laughed Henriette.

"That's right," continued Uncle Félix. "The plot thickens when the ghostly lady sends a mysterious message to the leading male character, Georges Brown, who wishes to buy the castle."

Before Uncle Félix could continue his summary, the gaslights began to dim and the audience hushed expectantly. Within moments, the orchestra began the overture and the curtain opened on a misty landscape which dimly revealed a towering château in the background. The audience broke into spontaneous applause and then settled into spellbound attention as the story unfolded. When the male protagonist became ensnared in a convoluted intrigue linking him to the secret of the castle, the curtain came down for intermission.

Henriette and Cécile left their mother sitting in the box with Uncle Félix while they sought out their friends in the foyer.

"Have you ever seen such an exciting opera?" queried Henriette when she found them.

"Never!" they all agreed. "And the soprano is perfect for the role, don't you think?" asked Cécile. "She seems so . . . ethereal."

"What do you think is going to happen?" Juliette wanted to know.

"I have no idea, but I do know I'm dying of thirst," said Henriette. "Let's go to the bar and get some punch," to which they all agreed.

"Your *maman* looks very beautiful tonight," Juliette said to Henriette and Cécile, "and she really seems to be enjoying herself."

"She's always loved opera and this is her first social outing in over a month," said Cécile. "I don't believe she's thought of anything else since we received M. Hart's invitation."

"I'm glad we could all be here together," said Henriette, smiling. Then on a more serious note she added, "I know you all realize that our *maman* is very high strung and that lately she's been having severe headaches—almost every day."

"Has she been to see a doctor?" Joséphine asked.

"Maman doesn't have much faith in doctors. She thinks they don't know as much as they'd like us to believe," said Cécile. "The one time she saw a doctor he told her she was suffering from nervous exhaustion. He said to get plenty of rest and not to go out in the hot sun. You can imagine how she reacted to that!"

"Well, I don't blame her," chimed in Juliette. "Anyone with common sense knows as much."

"When one of us is sick," Henriette added, "Maman makes a tisane from herbs growing in the garden. If we don't have any, she gets it from the garden behind the Ursuline convent."

As more people spilled into the foyer, the girls overheard a group of people speaking English.

"I didn't know Yankees liked opera!" said Cécile, looking surprised. "I wonder if they even know enough French to understand what's going on."

"I think some do," said Henriette, "but even if they don't, they probably enjoy the music."

"My papa says that many of them do speak French, and that we'd be surprised at how well educated some of the Yankees are," commented Joséphine.

"Well, I'm surprised to see them here at all," pursued Cécile. "They highly disapprove of our love of opera and theatre."

"No, it's mostly the balls they disapprove of," explained Joséphine, "and especially if they happen to take place on Sunday."

"Why shouldn't there be balls on Sunday?"

"Because they think it shows disrespect for the Sabbath," answered Joséphine.

"Really?" said Juliette, who until now had been quiet on the subject. "What do you think, Henriette? Does that show disrespect for the Sabbath?"

But Henriette merely smiled at her, for at that moment the ringing of the bell announced the end of intermission, calling everyone back into the theatre.

Soon the audience was settled and ready to watch the unfolding of the plot and enjoy the rest of the opera. Bit by bit they learned that *la dame blanche* wasn't a ghost at all but a very beguiling lady. When the final curtain came down to thunderous applause, everyone was smiling and cheering at the revealed identity of *la dame blanche* and the romantic outcome between her and Georges Brown. The applause continued through numerous curtain calls as people cheered, clapping and shouting, "Bravo, bravo!" When nearly everyone was hoarse, the applause died down and people filed out of the theatre.

In the cool evening breeze, laughter and farewells could be heard everywhere. Henriette, spying her friends, ran over and said, "Let's meet Sunday morning at the cathedral. After mass we can have *café au lait* in the square." They agreed and Henriette rejoined Cécile and her mother for the short walk home, Jefferson lighting the way.

Chapter 6

Rattlesnakes and Rheumatism

Sunday dawned bright and sunny over the French Quarter, promising another lovely spring day. Henriette walked the short distance from her house to St. Louis Cathedral, where she met Juliette and Joséphine before the nine o'clock mass. An hour later, the congregation poured out of the cathedral into the Place d'Armes, where spring breezes blew in from the Mississippi River. The redbud trees were in full bloom, and the scent of bridal wreath permeated the air. Robins, on their journey back north, sang from the treetops.

The three girls had planned to get piping-hot *café au lait* from the street vendor then sit on one of the benches in the square to reminisce over the opera. However, during mass they had noticed one of the oldest slaves in the Quarter slumped over in the pew, holding her head in her hands.

"Did you see poor old Sarah sitting in St. Joseph's side chapel?" asked Juliette. "She looks more frail and stooped every time I see her."

"Is she ill or is she just getting old? Maybe she shouldn't be coming to mass alone anymore," wondered Joséphine.

"There she is now coming out the side door," said Juliette. "She's having trouble getting down the steps."

"And she looks terribly weak," added Henriette. "Let's go offer to walk her home."

Sarah was bent over and leaning heavily on her cane. She appeared to be in pain with each step.

"*Bonjour*, Sarah," they called to her.

"*Tiens, bonjour, mes chères,*" replied Sarah, looking up to see their smiling faces. "Y'all looks mighty cheerful!"

"We're happy to see you, Sarah," replied Henriette, "and we've come to walk you home if you'd like our company."

"*Oh, mes chères,*" said Sarah, "I walks too slow. My rheumatism be hurtin' bad today."

"We're not in a hurry, Sarah. You just take all the time you need," Joséphine assured her.

Since she was a young girl Sarah had belonged to several generations of the Bosque family. No one knew for certain how old she was, but it was generally believed that she was nearing ninety. The girls could see how painful it was for her to maneuver. Joséphine and Henriette flanked Sarah on either side and Juliette followed as the little party made its way down Chartres Street. There wasn't much they could do to ease Sarah's pain, but their company lent moral support.

"Sarah, do you have any kind of medicine you can take for the pain?" Henriette inquired.

"The onliest thing I knows is put some warm rags where the pain be worst," replied Sarah sadly. "It he'p a li'l bit but it don' las' long. They say I gots to keep movin'. Tha's why I keeps comin' to church."

"My mother knows a lot about herbs and plant medicines," volunteered Henriette. "I'll ask her what's good for rheumatism."

"Bless you, chile, I's willin' to try anythin'," said Sarah with a sad little smile. "They ain't nobody at the French Market knows 'bout rheumatism. They say to go to the Indian market and they got somethin' there. But it be's too far 'way."

"I'll find out for you, Sarah. My mother will know what to do. I think she's even been to the Indian market to buy special herbs."

Eventually they arrived at the large colonial-style Bosque house on Chartres Street. As they said good-bye to Sarah, Henriette promised, "I'll let you know by tomorrow what my *maman* says."

"Bless you, chile. Not many young 'uns thinks 'bout makin' ol' Sarah feel better," she said, waving to them as she entered the gate.

"Let's go straight to my house," said Henriette, quickening her step. "I want to ask my *maman* if she can help Sarah."

"Do you think she'll do that for someone else's slave?" asked Juliette.

"We may have to convince her," answered Henriette. Then with a teasing little smile, she added, "I'm counting on the two of you to help me."

"We'll come with you, but you'll have to do the talking. Tell her how old Sarah is and how much she's suffering," offered Joséphine. "I'm sure she wouldn't refuse to help if she could see her."

"If she knows of a remedy, she'll tell us what it is. You can be sure of that," replied Henriette.

When they arrived at the house, they found Pouponne in the patio sipping her morning *café au lait* from a beautiful china cup. Nanou was clearing away the breakfast dishes. She and Pouponne looked surprised to see the three of them flushed and out of breath.

"I hope you girls haven't been running through the Quarter making a spectacle of yourselves," scolded Pouponne.

"*Non,* Maman, we weren't running but it's warm today and we were hurrying to ask if you know a remedy for rheumatism," replied Henriette.

"Rheumatism? There's no cure for that. Why do you want to know?" she asked, furrowing her brow. "It doesn't run in our family and I don't think any of our friends have it."

"But we know someone, Maman, and she's very old and suffers terribly from rheumatism."

"And who would that be?" queried Pouponne, suspicious of who her daughter had in mind.

"It's old Sarah. I told her how good you are with herbs and medicines and that you'd be able to help her."

"I should have known! You've been mingling with slaves

again," she said, frowning. "How many times must I tell you free people of color don't socialize with slaves?"

"Please, Maman, we saw Sarah in church. She's in so much pain that we offered to walk her home. Did you know she's practically ninety? You must know some remedy that would help her."

"Well, of course I do," she replied. "Willow-bark tea will ease any kind of pain but the best thing for rheumatism is rattlesnake grease rubbed where it hurts. Trouble is, it's hard to find."

"Oh!" responded Joséphine, suddenly very alert. "I bet that's why they told Sarah to go to the Indian market."

"That's right," said Pouponne, peering at her. "And did they also tell her it's hard to get and very expensive?"

"I don't know," said Joséphine, feeling intimidated.

"I don't think Sarah has any money," added Juliette.

"Well, I hope you girls aren't thinking of asking me to spend money on someone else's slave," said Pouponne, eyeing the three of them.

"How much does it cost?" asked Henriette, undaunted. "Maybe we could ask the Bosques to get it for Sarah."

"The cost is whatever the Indians want to ask," said Pouponne. "Do you think catching rattlesnakes is easy?"

"Where exactly is the Indian market?" Henriette, having once made up her mind to do something, became more determined in the face of obstacles.

"It's all the way out to Bayou St. John," responded Pouponne peevishly. "I've been there once or twice, but I have no intention of going again. What for? All the things I need I can get from the garden."

"Oh no, Maman, we weren't thinking of asking you to do that."

"And don't you get any ideas of going out there yourselves. It's too dangerous for young girls to be drifting that far out of the Quarter."

"*Non,* Maman, we won't. But thank you for the information. We'll try to find someone who can get that snake grease for Sarah."

Juliette and Joséphine also thanked Pouponne as the three of them slipped out of the patio, eager to return to the Place d'Armes. There, they settled on a park bench in the sun to enjoy their long-delayed *café au lait* and some beignets as well. They immediately began talking about Sarah, the rattlesnake grease, and the Indian market.

"Do you think your *maman* is right about the rattlesnake grease?" asked Josephine.

"Oh yes," said Henriette, "she knows a great deal about all kinds of remedies; they've been handed down for generations in our family."

"Could we ask the Bosques to buy medicine for Sarah?" asked Juliette, sounding doubtful.

"No, I don't think they'll listen to us," volunteered Joséphine. "If they haven't already done something for her, they're not going to do it because we ask them."

"I have another idea," said Henriette.

"Tell us," the other two chorused, looking hopeful.

"Well, I believe my Oncle Félix goes to the Indian market quite regularly with his wagon to get supplies. I bet he knows some Indians who could get what we need for Sarah."

"And will your Oncle Félix pay for the medicine too?" Joséphine questioned.

"Well, he might help pay for it, but Maman said it could be very expensive. I'll go see Oncle Félix tomorrow morning on my way to school and find out how much it will cost. Then we can take up a collection at school. Sister Ste Marthe will help us talk to the students. If each one gives just a little, we might be able to buy Sarah's rattlesnake grease."

"That's a wonderful idea," agreed Juliette.

"But some students may not be able to contribute," added Joséphine, thinking of how her own family depended on what she earned sewing baby clothes.

"You're right, Joséphine," said Henriette, who knew her family's situation. "But first, let's find out if we can even get it from the Indians. Then we'll decide how to pay for it. Besides,

Oncle Félix is very clever. He might have some other ideas."

Early the next morning Henriette stopped at Félix Delille's Grocery and Emporium. She found her uncle stacking bolts of white muslin which Jacques had brought from the wharf over the weekend.

"*Bonjour, mon oncle,*" she called. "Did you enjoy the opera on Friday as much as the first time you saw it?"

"Even more! I thought the singing was better this time and the story was delightful as always," he responded jovially. "What are you doing here so early on a Monday morning? Does your *maman* need something?"

"*Non,* not Maman. But someone else needs something very badly."

"And do I know this 'someone else'?" He cocked his head, giving her a sidelong glance as he lit his pipe.

"It's old Sarah who belongs to the Bosques," she explained. "I'm sure you know her, Oncle Félix."

"Yes, of course," he said, drawing heavily to inhale the tobacco fumes. "Sarah's been living in the Quarter as long as I can remember. She used to make fancy cloth shoes to match ladies' ball gowns," he said, reminiscing.

"I didn't know that. Where did she learn how?"

"I believe it was at the French Market from one of the slaves who escaped from Saint Domingue. Sarah was young then and got to be real good at it. Before long she was selling fancy slippers all over the Quarter."

"Didn't the Bosques object?" Henriette inquired.

"No indeed. She helped support the family with the money she made. She also saved a goodly amount from profits the Bosques let her keep. She was planning to buy her freedom but changed her mind when she got old and realized she didn't have family close by."

"Do you think Sarah still has money?"

"I think it's quite likely."

"My friends and I saw her yesterday at mass. She told us how she suffers from rheumatism. Maman says the only thing good for that is rattlesnake grease, but you can only find it at the Indian market," she explained.

"Aha, now I see what you're driving at," he said, catching on to his clever niece. "You want me to go to the Indian market and get some of that snake oil for you." His eyes twinkled and he tried to suppress a smile.

"Exactly!" she said, beaming and interpreting his demeanor as willingness to cooperate. "Will you be going soon?" she asked.

"Hmnn . . . Well, I don't usually go that often and it's too early in the season for Indian corn. I suppose I could use a couple of leather deer hides, and there's always a market for the baskets they weave from cane. Those Indians grind up sassafras leaves to make the best gumbo filé you can find. Could maybe pick some up since my supply is running low."

Henriette, knowing her uncle liked to tease, sensed that he was putting her off. "But, *mon oncle,* what about the rattlesnake grease?" she interrupted, pulling him back to the subject at hand. "Will you get some for Sarah?"

"Well, I never have bought any of their snake oil but I suppose they usually have it."

"Maman says it's expensive. That's why I was asking if Sarah still has some money. I think the girls at school will help pay for it, but I'm not sure how much we can collect."

Oncle Félix silently drew on his pipe, deliberating over what his niece had told him. Then, looking directly at Henriette, he said, "I'll talk to the Indians. They probably know how much of this stuff you need to feel better. Maybe a little bit is enough. If it's not more than five dollars, I'll go ahead and get it. You can pay me back later."

"Oh, *merci beaucoup.* I knew you'd find a way to help us!" Henriette's enthusiasm revived at her uncle's willingness to help. "Sarah will be so grateful. Can you go to the Indian market tomorrow?"

"My, my, but you are a go-getter," he laughed. "I can do

better than that. I'll drive out there this afternoon; I usually close up early on Mondays anyway. If they have it I'll bring it back with me this evening."

Henriette was beside herself with joy. She threw her arms around her uncle's neck and gave him a big hug and a kiss. Dashing out of the store, she turned and called out, "I'll be back this evening before dark to get that rattlesnake grease." With that, she ran off to share her joy with her friends, leaving Uncle Félix shaking his head.

True to her word, Henriette returned to her uncle's store just as the evening Angelus was ringing from the neighboring churches. Could it be a good omen that Uncle Félix had found the snake oil? she wondered

He smiled when he told her that he had obtained a large snakeskin pouch of the rattlesnake grease from one of the Indians he often traded with. "And I got it for a bargain—five dollars—exactly what I agreed to put up." He grinned as he held out the precious ointment.

A half-hour later Henriette placed the container in Sarah's trembling hands. She looked at Henriette in disbelief. Her face was like that of a child struck with awe. "Mlle Henriette, I can't believe how fast you gets this for me. I's been hearin' 'bout dis miracle cure for two or three years and here you gets it for me in one day. You the one be's the miracle!"

"My Oncle Félix deserves the credit. He got it from the Indians for five dollars. We'll take up a collection at school to pay him back."

"Wait," said Sarah, beaming. She took a little leather purse from around her neck, opened it, and painstakingly counted out five dollars in change. "I's been savin' money for years to buy my freedom. And sho nuff I be's buyin' my freedom— from rheumatism!" She laughed and cried at the same time as she hugged and thanked Henriette.

Henriette was so overcome that she felt a big lump in her throat and her eyes welled with tears. She had no idea what rheumatism felt like, but it must be bad if Sarah was so happy at the mere thought of getting relief. She walked home with a heart full of joy, remembering something Sister Ste Marthe had once told them. Now she understood the quotation: "It is more blessed to give than to receive."

Chapter 7

Yellow Jack and Yankee Invasion

The year 1829 was not the worst year for yellow fever in New Orleans, but when an English sea captain on a first visit to the city came down with the disease in June of that year, anxiety took hold in almost every household in the French Quarter. New Orleanians who had not already left for the somewhat cooler weather of the Gulf Coast in Mississippi or the pine forests on the north shore of Lake Pontchartrain began to think of fleeing the city, at least those who were prosperous enough to do so.

"I hope this won't be a bad year," said Cécile, who came home from shopping one day with the news that several other cases of the fever had been reported.

The mood was somber as the family sat down to dinner. "Remember that terrible epidemic we had a few years ago? More than two thousand people died," Cécile recalled, shuddering as she thought of the hearses and makeshift wagons that rattled through the city, their drivers shouting, "Bring out your dead!"

"They didn't have enough room in the cemetery to bury all the bodies," added Henriette. "People still talk about how horrible the smell was all over . . ."

"That's enough of that kind of talk," Pouponne interrupted sharply.

"Well, I'm worried about the baby," Cécile said. "And Antoinette, too."

Cécile's new baby was only four months old and it was well

known that the very young and the very old were especially susceptible to the disease.

"Do you think M. Hart would take the little ones to the Gulf Coast for safety?" she asked her mother.

"Don't worry about them," Pouponne assured her. "You know as well as I do that we who've lived here so long are used to the climate and conditions in the city. The fever doesn't affect us. The children will be fine," she said confidently.

"Jean's already in the country at St. Martinville, so he's certainly safe," said Henriette. She, too, felt that she was immune to the dreaded fever.

In the weeks ahead as reports spread of more victims and more deaths, she began to ponder ways that she, Juliette, and Joséphine might help those who were stricken. They had already been praised for their service to the poor and the sick, particularly by Père Antoine, who called them "God's angels."

The city soon set about its usual response to a possible epidemic. Large containers of tar were placed on street corners and set afire, producing an acrid smoke which was thought to drive away the "miasma" in the air which many believed caused the deadly disease. And at regular intervals throughout the day, cannons were fired from the Place d'Armes.

"I wish they wouldn't fire those cannons," complained Henriette, holding her ears as she returned home one day from school. "Do you think it does any good, Maman?"

"No, my Henriette. They think the noise from the cannons clears the atmosphere." She snorted. "Probably all that smoke makes it worse."

"What's the cure for yellow jack, Maman? Not everyone dies of it."

"The best treatment is a bath of tepid water several times a day, good broth if the patient can swallow, and lots of rest." Pouponne was confident of this treatment, which had been handed down in her family for generations.

"Sister Ste Marthe said they gave that sea captain doses of

mercury and splashed him with cold water," said Henriette.

"Huh," her mother sneered. "The mercury probably killed him before the yellow jack got him. It must have been one of those stupid American doctors he had. They think they know so much. The Yankees," she added, "they're the ones who have the most to fear. And anyone else who comes here from away, like that English sea captain."

Pouponne's opinion was widespread among the Creoles. They even called the fever "the strangers' disease." And to some extent it was true. The majority of victims were newcomers to the city, whether Americans who were flocking to New Orleans for reasons of commerce or the French fleeing unrest in their native country.

"Maman," interjected Henriette, "Sister Ste Marthe told me that two of M. Landry's slaves have come down with the fever."

"Hardly any slaves die of the fever—unless they're from away. They'll probably be all right."

"But the whole Landry family's gone to the Gulf Coast. Who'll take care of them?" Henriette continued.

"Well, I'm sure I don't know," Pouponne retorted. "That's the Landrys' problem."

"Shouldn't we try to do something for them?" Henriette dared to ask. "I could go see them."

"It's none of our business. What do you want to do—make yourself the servant of slaves?"

The next morning while having coffee at the French Market with Juliette and Joséphine, Henriette told them about the Landrys' slaves.

"I think we ought to go to the Landrys' and see how they are. Maybe we could help them."

Juliette and Josephine nodded. Sister Ste Marthe often told them of sick slave children and poor elderly blacks who needed help.

"We could bring them some soup," Henriette suggested. "I'll ask Nanou to put some aside for them. I'm sure she will." She gave them a meaningful look.

Juliette and Joséphine knew what she meant. The soup would be a secret between Henriette and Nanou, for Pouponne certainly would not approve of their attending other people's slaves. They agreed to meet after lunch.

However, when Henriette got home she discovered that Pouponne was about to leave to visit Uncle Felix. It was a hot, sunny day and when she took her parasol from the stand by the door and opened it, one of the metal ribs gave a pinging sound and cracked in two.

"What a bother!" she exclaimed. "I can't go without my parasol. I'll die of the heat. Henriette, you must take it to the umbrella shop for me at once. I'm sure they can fix it right away."

"But Maman, I was going to take Antoinette for a walk . . ."

Her mother interrupted her with a peremptory, "You can do that later. This will take no time at all. Here, take some coins; it won't cost much." And she thrust some change into Henriette's hand.

"But where do I go, Maman? I don't know where the umbrella man is anymore."

"What do you mean? He's where he's always been—on Royal Street right off Conti."

"That's where all the Americans are now. We never go there."

"Well, I know M. Durel's umbrella shop is there as it has always been. Mathilde Labatt told me she went there last week to buy a new parasol."

Henriette still stood with a stricken look on her face. Her mother threw up her hands in exasperation and said, "Well, take Betsy with you if it'll make you feel any better. Americans may be crude and vulgar, but they won't eat you. Don't pay any attention to them."

Pouponne went to the kitchen to fetch Betsy, and Henriette appealed to her sister for help. But Cécile merely shrugged her shoulders. "There's no talking reason to Maman these days. She'll get all upset if you don't do just as she says."

In a few moments Betsy appeared and followed Henriette

to the door. Away they went, with Betsy walking a pace behind. "Why don't you walk with me and hold my hand?" pleaded Henriette as they rounded the corner heading toward Royal Street.

Betsy frowned. "Miss Henriette, ah don' think so. What would yo' *maman* say?"

Henriette sighed, but as they strolled farther along Royal she gave all her attention to the shops on both sides of the street, every one of which had signs not in French but in English. The storefronts were freshly painted and the entryways swept clean.

"Oh look, Betsy," Henriette gasped as she stopped at one store, gawking at its elaborate display of heirloom jewels— necklaces, earrings, bracelets, and rings. The sign above the entrance proclaimed, "Waldorf's Jewels for All Occasions."

"Jes look at dat," said Betsy as they stood side by side ogling the sparkling display, until Henriette took her by the hand and pulled her along.

Just two doors down was M. Durel's umbrella shop, identified by the open umbrella hanging upside down from a pole above the entrance. "Well, Maman was right. It's still here. But everything else looks so different."

Henriette had not been in this part of the city in a long time. Now so many American businesses had displaced Creole tenants that she hardly recognized the neighborhood. With relief they saw that the umbrella shop still had its French sign: *"Parapluies réparés ici."*

"It looks so sad," exclaimed Henriette as they noticed how old and shabby the shop appeared next to its newer neighbors.

"Huh! Looks like M. Durel needs to do a li'l paintin' and fixin' up," muttered Betsy.

Henriette strode into the dark interior, located the elderly proprietor, and showed him Pouponne's parasol. He took a quick look at it and said he could repair it while they waited.

"Are there many Creole shops left around here?" Henriette inquired.

"Oh, no, *mademoiselle*. Mine is one of the few. The Americans came with their new way of doing things—very fast, you know—and most of my neighbors sold out to them. The Americans, all they're interested in is making money. Things are not the same as they used to be." He added sadly, "I guess one day soon, I'll have to move out too. I don't know where I'll go."

He took the parasol into a little back room to repair it. Since there was no place to sit and Henriette's curiosity was getting the better of her, she and Betsy went outside and walked up Royal toward Canal Street, inspecting shop windows and businesses. Occasional passersby looked curiously at the attractive Creole girl and her slave. Several men tipped their hats and Henriette nodded politely, but for the most part she was engrossed in studying the storefronts and their English signs.

"Look across the street." She gently nudged Betsy with her elbow, not wishing to point. "There's where M. Touzet's cabinet shop used to be. It's something else now." The newly painted sign above the entrance said, "Ladies' Embroidery and Sewing Supplies." As they looked, two women came out of the store chattering in English, but Henriette understood not a word of it.

"Betsy, did you know there were so many Americans here? We hardly ever see them in our part of the Quarter."

"Da's jus' fine wit' me," said Betsy, feeling uncomfortable in this unfamiliar territory. "We's better git back to da umbrella man."

And so they returned to M. Durel, who had Pouponne's parasol fixed as good as new, which he demonstrated by opening and closing it several times. Henriette thanked him politely and handed him his fee. Then she and Betsy were back on the street, heading toward home. But not the way they had come.

Betsy protested, "What you doin'? Ain't we goin' home?" She grabbed Henriette by the arm.

"Yes, we're going home, but straight down Royal a ways," Henriette insisted. "It's changed so much I want to see just how far the Americans have moved into the Quarter."

"Too far," declared Betsy.

Henriette slowed her steps as she looked across the street at a freshly painted shop with a sign in English above the entrance: "Hamilton's Haberdashery." The window displayed several suits of men's clothing and an assortment of men's hats. English signs continued until they got to Toulouse Street, where the stores bore familiar signs in French. Now they felt more comfortable, back in their own part of town. Both Henriette and Betsy, hearing their familiar French, relaxed. They passed well-known landmarks and as they caught sight of the steeple of St. Louis Cathedral they heard the day's first cannon volley from the Place d'Armes.

Henriette put her hands to her ears and turned to Betsy. "Oh, Betsy," she shouted, "that reminds me. We'll be back home in a few minutes. I know you heard about the two Landry slaves who've come down with the fever. Would you ask Nanou to make some beef broth for them?"

Betsy paused before she answered. "And what yo' Maman goin' to say to dat?"

"Well, Nanou could make some for us and then put some aside. No one has to say anything to Maman."

"Huh," was all Henriette heard from Betsy, but she knew that meant they understood one another.

When they got home Henriette handed her mother the repaired parasol and told her of the new American shops they had seen and how everyone on the street was speaking English.

"English! What's this city coming to?" lamented Pouponne. "Such an unpleasant sound that language makes." She told Henriette that Juliette and Joséphine had come looking for her and said they would meet her in front of the cathedral.

"Oh, yes, thank you, Maman," and she hurried back to

Nanou and asked her for some clean cloths that she might use to help in nursing the Landrys' slaves. In a few moments she was on her way and soon joined Juliette and Joséphine. Together they hurried to the Landrys' house on Dumaine and rang the bell on the gate. A young black boy came out looking fearful. He smiled in relief on seeing the three girls.

"You're Etienne, aren't you? Where are the sick ones and how many are there?" Henriette asked.

"There be's two—in da slave quarter," he answered, pointing to the back patio.

"Take us there; we want to help."

Etienne opened the gate and they all hurried down the alley.

"What's their condition?" Henriette asked on the way. "Have they vomited very much, is there any bleeding?"

"Dey cain't eat nothin'," he answered, "and li'l Henri, he be's bleedin' from da nose all mornin'."

"Is there anyone else here to help?" asked Juliette. "Isn't there a handyman—Jessie, I think?"

The boy shook his head. "Dey took Jessie along wid 'em. Jes me an' dem." As they entered the small building, he pointed to the two figures lying next to each other on cots covered with dirty, blood-stained sheets. One was a young boy about eight or nine years old and the other an elderly woman who was moaning and rubbing her face. The boy's nose oozed blood, which he wiped away with his bare hand.

Pointing to the woman Henriette said, "That must be Marie Rose. She came from Saint Domingue many years ago." She turned to the houseboy. "Quick, get us some water from the cistern. If it's cold, make a fire and heat it, not hot, just warm. Now hurry," and she gave him a little shove. She handed a cloth to Juliette and told her to wipe the boy's face. She directed Joséphine to raise the old woman's head so they could dry her forehead, which was glistening with sweat.

"How could the Landrys leave them here like this with no help?" asked Joséphine. "I thought they were nice people. I see them in church every Sunday."

Henriette shrugged her shoulders. "People are so afraid of the fever. I guess that makes them do things they wouldn't ordinarily do."

The three girls rearranged the bedclothes and made the sick ones as comfortable as possible. When Etienne returned with a basin of warm water they gently bathed their patients. The old woman stopped moaning and seemed to relax as Henriette hummed a soothing melody in her ear.

"Do you think it would do any good to put a string of garlic around their necks?" whispered Joséphine. "People say that's a good treatment."

"No, Joséphine, people do that to stop from getting the fever, but my *maman* says once they've got it nothing helps but what we're doing. How I wish I had that broth right now." She questioned little Etienne, "Do you have any soup in the kitchen?"

"No'm. We got some bananas and bread, an' I can get some eggs from da henhouse."

"No, that won't do. I'll come back later with some broth."

The dinner hour was fast approaching and the girls knew their families would be expecting them. Henriette and Juliette promised to return later but Joséphine said her mother needed her at home the rest of the afternoon. "Don't worry, Joséphine. We understand," Henriette assured her. "Juliette and I can handle it." Joséphine's mother was making it more and more difficult for her daughter to join her friends. Henriette knew that if her own mother could see her daughter now, she too would be furious, for Pouponne suspected that somehow Henriette's good works were related to her reluctance to attend all the balls as her sister had done.

Henriette told Etienne to continue tending the patients by bathing their faces and arms with warm water and to try to find some fresh bedclothes for them. Juliette volunteered to stay long enough to show Etienne how to bathe the patients properly.

"Where's Henri's mother?" she asked Etienne after the others had left.

"She be's in da country wit' da Landrys," he answered. "M. Landry's *maman* be sick and Henri's *maman,* she good at he'pin' out."

"I wish she were here to help out," she said to herself as she wiped Henri's nose.

At home, Henriette hurried to the kitchen to wash up and ask Nanou about the broth. As soon as Nanou saw her, she shook her head. "Ah knows what you want. Ah gots a good beef broth goin' but it take time."

"I can't go back till after dinner, Nanou. It should be ready by then, don't you think?"

"Maybe," said Nanou, pouring a pot full of shrimp stew into a large tureen. "Look here, take dat rice in to da table. Tell your *maman* I be right der soon as I git da cornbread out da oven."

Luckily for Henriette, most of the attention throughout the meal was directed to Antoinette, who was amusing everyone by making funny faces at her baby brother and rolling her big brown eyes round and round.

"That's enough of that," Pouponne said and rose from her chair abruptly. "I have a headache and I'm going upstairs to lie down for a while."

Just then they heard a knock at the door. It was Uncle Félix, who bore the disturbing news that Père Antoine had taken seriously ill and asked that they pray for his recovery.

"Mon Dieu," exclaimed Pouponne, making the sign of the cross, then striking her breast several times. "You go to the cathedral so much, Henriette. Go there now and pray for our beloved friend."

On her way back to the Landrys', Henriette stopped at the cathedral, carefully guarding the broth Nanou had given her as she prayed for Père Antoine. For several days thereafter she, Juliette, and sometimes Joséphine cared for young Henri and Marie Rose. The invalids gradually improved, gaining strength little by little. The girls were overjoyed at their recovery, but their joy was short lived, for they heard a few days later that Père Antoine, their beloved priest, had died at the age of eighty-one. As long as Henriette could remember, Père Antoine had been a presence in the Creole community. Sometimes he had been bitterly criticized, but for the most part he was revered by all the white Creole establishment, the free people of color, and the slaves, who benefited from his compassion and sympathy. Henriette admired him especially for his devotion to the sick and the imprisoned. She had often seen his brown-robed, hooded figure heading into the calaboose, the filthy prison next door to the cathedral.

Over the years, Pouponne had extolled him to Henriette and Cécile as a "real" priest. Henriette suspected that her mother was partial to the friar because of his tolerance of the alliances between white men and free women of color. It was widely believed that he had secretly married a number of interracial couples. Pouponne now declared that Père Antoine was a saint. She spent long hours at the cathedral, where his body lay in state for three days before his funeral. All the city's dignitaries and most of its citizens came to mourn him.

A large black crepe hung over Pouponne Diaz' front door for thirty days and Pouponne's sieges of depression became more frequent and more intense.

Chapter 8

The Big Splash

1832

After the death of Père Antoine, Henriette, Juliette, and Joséphine continued to volunteer at the St. Claude School. The enrollment had grown to such a number that it was becoming a problem. One Friday after class, Sister Ste Marthe asked the three of them to step into her classroom.

"My dear friends, I don't know what I would do without you. I'm getting on in years, you know, so your help has been invaluable to me. But, quite frankly, I can't pay any more full-time teachers because we're running out of money. I'm afraid the school may have to close."

The three young women looked at her in disbelief. "We can't let that happen," said Henriette. "St. Claude's is the only school for girls of mixed race. The Ursulines can't take them at the academy."

"I know. So I've decided to go back to France to get help," she said.

"You mean you're going to leave us?" asked Juliette. "But what will happen while you're gone?"

"Don't worry. I've arranged with the Ursulines for Sister François to replace me. Even if our girls can't attend Ursuline, there's no law to prevent the nuns from coming here to teach."

"It won't be the same without you," murmured Joséphine.

"Everything will be fine, but promise me you'll continue

teaching the little slave children. Sister François will depend on you for that."

"Of course we will," chimed the three of them.

A few weeks later, with smiles and tears, they embraced their beloved Sister Ste Marthe as she bade them farewell and boarded the ship that would return her to her native country. Months passed before they had word of her. And then one day in early fall, Sister François called the teachers together and announced, "I have good news. Sister Ste Marthe has arranged for more funding and for someone very special to come and direct St. Claude's School."

Everyone was delighted and wanted to know who it would be. "You'll never guess," she teased, trying to suppress a smile.

"Oh, please tell us. Do we know her? What city is she from?" they asked excitedly.

"She's already left France on a ship coming from La Rochelle," she answered. Then Sister François, trying to keep from smiling too broadly, surprised them by announcing, "It's my very own sister, Mlle Marie-Jeanne Aliquot!" Everyone burst into joyful chatter, clapping at the good news. Sister François would be reunited with her sister, and the future of St. Claude's School would be assured.

"Will Sister Ste Marthe be coming with her?" Henriette wanted to know.

"I'm afraid not. She's not been well lately. We don't know when she'll be returning." Although this saddened the girls, it did not surprise them. They remembered how thin and pale Sister looked when they last saw her before she sailed for France. She had worn herself out by years of working in New Orleans.

"Read the daily *Courrier* to find out when the ship from France will arrive," Sister François told them as she ended the meeting.

And so it happened that in the December 4 edition of the *Courrier,* headlines on the front page announced that the ship *L'Haves* had arrived at the mouth of the Mississippi River and would dock in New Orleans in two days. Among the passengers' names they easily found that of Mlle Marie-

Jeanne Aliquot. Sister François decided to suspend classes on December 6 in anticipation of her sister's arrival.

That morning the three girls made their way toward the riverfront. Activity on the wharf was always bustling, but a passenger ship arriving from France was a festive occasion. As they approached the landing site, officious looking businessmen in frock coats, hatted ladies in carriages, excited Ursuline nuns in starched white wimples, and men, women, and children of every skin tone anxiously congregated to watch the ship dock and to welcome its passengers. Numerous slaves were on hand to tote the heavy luggage. Within a short time they heard a loud blast from the ship's horn, announcing its arrival.

"Juliette, Joséphine, over here, by this piling," cried Henriette excitedly as she scrambled to stake out a spot for the three of them. "We can see everyone come down the ramp from here."

"Good idea," called Joséphine, following her friend's lead. "The stevedores won't let anyone get close to the dock. It's dangerous once they start throwing the mooring lines."

"Did you see Mlle Aliquot's name in the *Courrier?*" asked Juliette.

"Yes, at the top of the list," answered Joséphine. "She'll probably stay with her sister at the Ursuline Convent, don't you think?"

"I suppose, for a while," answered Juliette. "Sister François said she'll teach the class of older girls when school starts in January." She paused and added, "I heard that Mlle Aliquot is very rich. Is that true?"

But Henriette's and Joséphine's attention was elsewhere. "Look," cried Joséphine excitedly, "you can see the ship rounding the bend in the river!"

As soon as the ship came into view a cheer burst from the crowd. Throngs of people surged forward to catch a glimpse of friends and family on board. From the riverbank, Sister François pointed to the bow of the ship and said, "Oh, look, there she is—my sister—the one with the lovely blue bonnet."

On deck, Marie-Jeanne spied the bevy of religious habits and began vigorously fluttering her handkerchief. Everyone was waving, shouting, laughing, and crying tears of joy at the same time. Shrieks of welcome split the air. The three young women cheered and waved energetically with the rest of the crowd, but everyone hushed as the ship slowly inched toward the assigned spot at the wharf. At a signal from the captain, sailors on board threw lines to the stevedores on shore, who drew the ship toward the dock. Everyone breathed a sigh of relief when it finally came to rest a few feet from the wharf.

At that moment the crew on board went into action lowering the ramp. The longshoremen snatched it with grappling hooks and secured it to the dock. Passengers began slowly descending the stretch of makeshift walkway suspended in midair.

"It looks pretty scary to me," said Juliette, her eyes wide with apprehension. "I'm glad I'm not the one climbing off that ship."

"It does look a bit wobbly. You have to move slowly and hang on to the side rope. Otherwise you could lose your balance," explained Henriette.

The passengers came one by one or two by two, gentlemen holding ladies' hands to steady them. After carefully making their way down the long ramp, each passenger was welcomed warmly with hugs and kisses from eager friends and family. Finally Marie-Jeanne appeared in her blue bonnet, holding the hand rope and making her way gingerly down the walkway. She had not descended more than a third of the way when one of the passengers accidentally dropped a heavy footlocker onto the ramp. Before anyone could stop its progress, it veered sideways, plunging directly behind Marie-Jeanne. Several in the crowd, seeing what was about to happen, screamed and gestured frantically. "*Attention!*" "*Prenez garde!*" "Look out!" Marie-Jeanne, who had no idea what was happening, looked at the crowd, bewildered. Just then, the suitcase struck her from behind. She fell on top of the luggage, arms flailing, trying in vain to grasp the rope. Everyone watched in horror. Marie-Jeanne, together with the footlocker, hurtled sidelong under the handrail and into the murky waters below.

People screamed as they saw the slight body fall between the ship and the dock into the muddy river. They heard a splash. Then silence. The crowd peered into the river and saw nothing but a blue bonnet floating on the surface. Marie-Jeanne was nowhere in sight. "Help! Oh, dear God! Someone save her!" shouted the onlookers.

The nuns fell to their knees, praying, "Jesus, Mary, and Joseph, help us in our need. Our Lady of Prompt Succor, come to our aid." Sister François prayed most fervently, knowing her sister had never learned to swim. "Dearest Lord, please, please help!"

At that moment, Samuel, one of the biggest slaves from the stevedore crew, ran from behind a stack of cargo, dove into the murky waters, and swam to where the circular ripples were widening. He plunged beneath the surface and for several long moments was lost from sight. Then Marie-Jeanne reappeared, frantically thrashing about and gasping for air. But where was Samuel? Marie-Jeanne sank again as the crowd gasped. A full minute passed, seeming like an eternity, but still there was no sight of her. Finally, Samuel resurfaced toward the far end of the ship holding Marie-Jeanne's head above the water. "Look, there she is! Thank God! Is she still alive?" came voices from the crowd.

Samuel quickly swam toward the wharf and established a foothold on one of the pilings. Anxious hands reached down as he lifted Marie-Jeanne's limp body to them. They carefully laid her on the ground. A crowd gathered around the drenched figure but made way for the group of nuns who flocked to her side. Sister François knelt on the ground beside her sister, weeping and calling her name, "Marie-Jeanne, *ma chère* Marie-Jeanne."

Her body seemed lifeless as Sister François tapped her cheeks. Suddenly a tremor passed through the slight frame, causing Marie-Jeanne to cough and spit up some of the dirty brown water she had swallowed. "You're alive! Thank God, you're alive," cried Sister François, tears streaming down her face. The other nuns raised their hands to heaven in thanksgiving. Many onlookers did the same.

It was some time before Marie-Jeanne opened her eyes and struggled to speak. After minutes of coughing and gasping, she finally regained her breath. She looked up into Sister François' eyes. "Who saved me?" she whispered.

People began looking about for the burly slave who had risked his life to save hers. Somehow he had managed to hoist himself up the side of the wharf and from the edge of the crowd was waiting anxiously to see what would happen to the lady he had pulled from the muddy Mississippi.

"There he is," someone shouted, and the people made a wide path for him to approach.

"This is Samuel," said Sister François. "He's your rescuer, Marie-Jeanne."

"You saved my life," whispered Marie-Jeanne weakly. The big black man knelt humbly at her side. "How can I repay you?" she asked.

Samuel just shook his head from side to side, repeating, "Oh, no ma'am."

"Please come to the Ursuline Convent on Sunday, Samuel," said Sister François, Sunday being the day slaves were allowed to roam the Quarter. "My sister and I will want to speak to you when she's feeling better."

"Yaz'm" replied Samuel meekly.

The three friends had witnessed the entire drama. Like the other spectators, they were reviewing the series of rapid incidents that had led to the climax: the ship docking, the plunging footlocker, the big splash, and the fortunate, almost miraculous rescue. "Do you two know how lucky Mlle Aliquot is that Samuel found her?" asked Henriette, obviously stunned by what she had seen. "Most people who fall into the Mississippi are never seen again."

"Don't they ever come up for air?" asked Juliette.

"No, not in the Mississippi. They're caught by powerful undercurrents that sweep them out to sea."

"But we saw Mlle Aliquot come up, didn't we?" Joséphine wondered.

"I guess because she fell so close to the wharf. The ship must have acted as a barrier that kept her from being swept away by undercurrents," Henriette speculated.

"She and Samuel could have both been drowned down there." Juliette shuddered at the thought of such a tragedy.

"God must really want Mlle Aliquot to be in New Orleans. Maybe he has something special for her to do," mused Joséphine, a thoughtful look on her face.

Meanwhile, aboard *L'Haves,* a dismayed young lawyer from Tours gave thanks that the lady was all right, then grieved for the vanished footlocker that had held all his worldly goods. But surely his uncle in New Orleans would help him replace everything.

The following Sunday, Samuel appeared at the Ursuline convent, where Mlle Aliquot was expecting him. By this time she had recuperated almost completely from her harrowing experience. She and Sister François graciously shook Samuel's hand. He shyly reciprocated.

"You know, Samuel," said Sister François, looking directly at him, "it's thanks to you that my sister is alive today."

"Yes, Samuel, I believe God sent you to help me," added Marie-Jeanne.

"Yaz'm," he replied, looking at her with wide eyes. "Was God made me strong. He he'p me he'p you. Ah knows it."

"To show my gratitude, Samuel, I want you to know I'll always be ready to help you in any way I can," said Marie-Jeanne.

"You be's so kind, ma'am. Jes pray for me."

"Indeed I will, Samuel, and here's a small purse for you. But don't forget you can always call on me for help. If you need money or medicine or anything at all, you come and ask me."

"Thank you, ma'am. You be's mos' kind."

Within a week of meeting Samuel, Marie-Jeanne was conveniently settled in a small house near the Ursuline Convent, from where she could easily attend mass at the chapel. There was plenty of time before classes resumed in

January to explore New Orleans, the city founded in 1718 by her fellow countryman, Sieur de Bienville, more than a hundred years earlier. Never had she seen such a mix of races nor heard so many different languages in one place. Besides Creoles speaking French, she heard Spanish from descendants of Spanish rulers, pale-faced Americans speaking English, and African slaves speaking "gumbo" French. The faces she saw in the city ranged in color from black to brown to the fairest creamy complexion. Finally, she saw for the first time real American Indians—*les peaux rouges*—which she had heard about in France. Theirs was the strangest-sounding language of all.

Every time Marie-Jeanne left her house she had a new adventure. Walking toward the Place d'Armes and the cathedral she saw peddlers carrying baskets or pushing carts laden with delicious-smelling breads, cakes, fruits, vegetables, and wares of every kind. Cries of *"Calas, calas, tout chaud"* and *"Bel pam pa-tates, bel pam pa-tates"* tempted her to try some of the hot rice cakes and sweet potato patties sold by black women. Drawn by offers of *café au lait* and the pervasive aroma of the freshly brewed New Orleans coffee, she never missed a chance to buy a small cup of the delicious beverage. Marie-Jeanne delighted in the sights and sounds and even smells of this strange and wonderful city.

Observant as she was, she also became aware of many of the problems plaguing New Orleans. Instinctively she avoided the grinning hawkers who called out loudly from open doorways, "Come on in! Have some fun!" She told Sister François that on one such occasion, curiosity made her peer inside the dimly lit establishment. "I just barely made out men, and even some women, drinking, gambling, and laughing raucously right in the middle of the day. The women were dressed in red and someone was strumming a tinny banjo in the background. Heaven only knows what else was going on in there." Out in the open, the shocking spectacle of the slave market and harsh treatment by some of the slave owners shook Marie-Jeanne to the core. She felt within her a sudden rage that she had never experienced before. She thought of Samuel, who had saved her from drowning. With wonder and gratitude she prayed, "Dear Lord, I want to help slaves, but I don't know how to do that. Please show me a way."

After each venture into the Quarter, Marie-Jeanne peppered her sister with questions about the city, the people, and the school where she would be teaching. Sister François, speaking of the school's persistent financial troubles, said, "I'm sure you know that's why Sister Ste Marthe recruited you in France. Fortunately, we have three young women who volunteer their time teaching the slave children."

"Are those the three young ladies I've seen together in the chapel?"

"Yes, they're very special," answered Sister François. "They have worked with Sister Ste Marthe a long time. Like her, they're completely dedicated and do good things for all kinds of people, including slaves."

At the mention of slaves, Marie-Jeanne's eyes widened. "Do they?" she asked. "Tell me, where do they live?"

"Oh, they each live at home. Their families depend on them. In Henriette's case, her mother has been ailing for some time."

"She's ill?" asked Marie-Jeanne.

"Well, you could say that. But her illness is more mental than physical. People have always considered her eccentric. Lately, however, she acts so irrational that at times the girls can hardly deal with her. People say she once tried to sell a house that doesn't exist."

"Good heavens, that does sound bizarre," exclaimed Marie-Jeanne.

"I know. It finally got so serious that Cécile, Henriette's older sister, sent for their brother, Jean, who lives in St. Martinville. He came to help them decide what to do. They consulted their lawyer, who advised, for legal reasons, to have their mother interdicted, which meant she could no longer buy or sell any property. They were all very sad to do that but knew it was for the best."

"I gather then that Cécile and Henriette live in their mother's house?"

"They live together, but it's actually Cécile's house. She lives there with her four children. A certain M. Hart is the father, and I hear he's been ailing too."

"It all sounds rather complicated," said Marie-Jeanne, looking a bit mystified. "Does Henriette have any other brothers or sisters?"

"No, it's just the two girls and Jean. He's married and the family doesn't see him often since he now lives in St. Martinville with his wife and children."

"I see. Tell me more. What about her two friends?" urged Marie-Jeanne.

"I think they'd all like to become nuns, but Louisiana law forbids mixed races from marrying or even living together. That law prevents the girls from joining a white community."

"A law you say? It can't be!" said Marie-Jeanne, looking puzzled.

"Well, it is. And in New Orleans the Americans enforce the law. Since they started moving into the city, lots of things have changed, especially between the races. When the Spanish ruled, the men who took slave mistresses freed them so their children wouldn't grow up in slavery. That's one reason we have so many free people of color in this city."

"But all this time I thought the girls were white," said Marie-Jeanne, astonished.

"True, most people would never guess they're descended from mixed parentage somewhere along the line. What's unusual is that these three light-skinned women never hesitate to identify with even the darkest slave. Most free people of color have nothing to do with slaves unless they own them. Henriette and her friends, on the other hand, look for ways to help any and all slaves. Their families strongly disapprove of this, especially Henriette's mother."

"And what about the other two girls?"

"Joséphine's parents are married free people of color.

Naturally, they want her to marry as well. She's very alert and clever with her hands. Her needlework is in great demand and she helps support the family with it."

"What does she do? Embroidery?"

"That, and she also sews beautiful clothes, including fine baby layettes."

"And what about Juliette?"

"Juliette is relatively free to do as she likes. No siblings. Her father is French and her mother a free woman of color. They were married in Saint Domingue and fled the revolution when Juliette was a baby."

"I'd like to meet these girls," said Marie-Jeanne, becoming more interested as she heard their stories.

"They want to meet you too. If you would like, I could invite them to come to the convent."

"Yes, please do."

"Good. I'll arrange it then," agreed Sister François.

Around three in the afternoon the following day, Henriette, Juliette, and Joséphine rang the Ursuline Convent bell. Sister François led them to the parlor and introduced them to her sister then excused herself to give them a chance to get acquainted. Marie-Jeanne plied them with questions. Did they always work together? How did they find people in need? Was it true they were willing to help anyone?

"We started by helping Sister Ste Marthe," explained Joséphine. "Our parents weren't happy about it, but we knew Sister couldn't do it all alone."

"Some day, when our families no longer need us," volunteered Henriette, "we might live together, but for now we work with the slave children and bring food and clothes to old folks."

"Sometimes we take care of sick people," added Joséphine, "and we have friends who help us from time to time."

"I want to help you too," said Marie-Jeanne decidedly. "Do you remember the day I arrived in New Orleans and nearly drowned?"

"We were there. We saw the whole thing!" cried the girls.

"Well, I realized that God must have saved me for a reason."

"That's the very thought I had when Samuel fished you out of the river," said Joséphine.

"You will be helping a lot just by teaching at our school," said Juliette.

"The problem is that the school has no money," explained Joséphine, "and no one knows how much longer it can keep going."

"Sister Ste Marthe told me as much," Marie-Jeanne said, nodding her head. "And I just learned that the property where the school is located has been sold."

"What? Sold?" the three of them echoed.

"What's to become of all the students?" queried Henriette, wide-eyed with astonishment. "There's no other school where girls of color can get an education. It's different for boys; many of them are sent to schools in France."

"And we can't forget the slave children who come for catechism," said Juliette.

"Please don't panic, girls. There may be a way out of this problem," said Marie-Jeanne, trying to reassure them. "There's a piece of property for sale in the Faubourg Tremé."

"We know the property," said Henriette, "but it's very expensive. No one wants to spend that much money to educate colored children."

"I do," smiled Marie-Jeanne.

"But can you afford it?" asked Joséphine.

"Yes, I can. When my father passed away two years ago, I inherited a large estate. I have since been wondering how to use the money for something good. When Sister Ste Marthe told me about her school in New Orleans, which was in need of funds, I knew immediately I had found my answer."

The three of them stared at her uncomprehendingly. "Were you a teacher in France when Sister Ste Marthe met you?" Juliette wanted to know.

"Yes, I've been teaching for a long time. You see, more than ten years ago I was engaged to be married, but my fiancé was killed in a hunting accident."

"Oh, that is so tragic. But didn't you ever think of marrying someone else?" Henriette asked.

"No. My fiancé was the love of my life. When I lost him I knew no one else could take his place. Since then, I have felt that God wants me to be useful in other ways."

"And now, God has sent you to us. It all fits together like the pieces of a puzzle," said Henriette. "Don't you agree?"

"Yes, I think you're right," said Marie-Jeanne. "My dear new friends, pray that I was sent here to do God's will." Then, coming back to the business at hand, she added, "Sister François knows of my desire to work for slaves. She disclosed to me that eventually the Ursulines might be willing to buy St. Claude's. First, however, I need to find a building and make sure the school is operating as smoothly as it was before Sister Ste Marthe left. For the time being, that is my main mission."

The girls were amazed. They had never met a white person, other than nuns and priests, so willing to help black people. Marie-Jeanne suddenly became their heroine. They felt instinctively that she would be their most loyal advocate.

When Sister François rejoined them in the parlor, they were still chattering feverishly about the recent developments and how they would affect the future.

"I knew you'd find plenty of things to talk about," she smiled. "I'm sorry, but I have to put you all out now. It's almost prayer time for the nuns."

"That's fine," laughed Marie-Jeanne. "We'll leave together and the girls can walk me home." They all agreed and rose to go.

Through the ensuing weeks the young women met frequently to discuss plans for the school. Marie-Jeanne was able to negotiate a sale and soon the property would be hers. Henriette admired Marie-Jeanne's fearlessness and generosity. Marie-Jeanne, on the other hand, marveled at the dedication and perseverance of these three young women in spite of opposition from their families.

The big splash made by Marie-Jeanne on her arrival in New Orleans was to create rippling waves in the years ahead.

Chapter 9

Voodoo and Visions of the Future

In the following months Marie-Jeanne met regularly with her young friends to discuss ways she could work with them to improve the lot of the slaves. Her enthusiasm added strength to the girls' determination to continue the mission that Sister Ste Marthe had first inspired them to follow. Gradually they were being pulled from the closeness of their family ties to a different allegiance. Henriette's Uncle Félix noticed this change in her focus, as did her brother, Jean, on his occasional visits from St. Martinville to New Orleans.

One Sunday after mass as Henriette was leaving the cathedral she heard a familiar voice. "Henriette, where are you going in such a hurry?" It was Uncle Félix.

"*Ah, Oncle Félix.*" She smiled as he gave her a quick hug and took her by the hand.

"I haven't seen much of you lately," he said. "I know you and Cécile are having a very bad time with Pouponne. You need a little diversion. How about going to Congo Square with me today for a little while?"

"*Ah, je ne sais pas, mon oncle,*" she murmured in confusion. "I seldom go there, you know. I don't like the voodoo dancing and all the drums."

"I know it's not as elegant as the opera, but sometimes it's amusing. And I would love to have some company. I don't see you very often these days."

Henriette bit her lip as she thought what to do. She loved her uncle and wanted to please him. "Oh," she looked up suddenly, a light in her eye. "I wonder if we could take little Samuel and Antoinette. It would give Cécile an easier time this afternoon."

"Why, that's a great idea, Henriette. I'll come by for you and the little ones right after dinner."

The children were excited at the prospect of an outing and were waiting at the gate for Uncle Félix when he came striding up the street that afternoon. The family walked toward Rampart Street and as they neared the square they heard drumbeats and chanting. The iron fence around the square was lined with well-dressed men and women looking at the scene within. A cluster of rough-looking flatboatmen were at the corner talking and laughing raucously, pointing at some of the dancers.

Henriette, Uncle Félix, and the children found an open spot away from the flatboatmen. The square was filled with slaves dressed in castoff Sunday finery provided by their masters and mistresses. In one corner a group of drummers kept up a steady beat while a circle of dancers with metal rattles on their legs twirled and high-stepped around, shaking and raising their arms to the sky.

"I think that's the bamboula they're dancing or maybe it's the calinda," said Uncle Félix.

"What are they singing?" Antoinette asked. "I don't understand the words."

"I don't either, Antoinette. It's some African tongue the slaves from Saint Domingue brought with them. Mandingo, I think."

Suddenly the chanting rose to a crescendo, then quickly dropped to almost a whisper. A high-pitched song burst forth from the figure in the circle of dancers, a tall quadroon woman dressed in the finest gown of all, red satin with a purple flounce at the bottom and a matching ruffle at the low-cut bodice. A long chain with a pendant shaped like a snake hung from her neck and in her hands she held a real live, writhing green snake.

"Oh," squealed Antoinette, "look, look, Oncle Félix, a snake! Is it real? Is it going to bite her?"

Uncle Félix laughed. "No, no, Antoinette, you don't have to worry. It's just a garter snake; some people have them for pets. It's not poisonous."

"I bet I could hold a snake," boasted Samuel.

"Oh," exclaimed Henriette. "I know that woman, Oncle Félix. She's one of the seamstresses at the dressmaker Maman likes so much. What is she doing here? She's not a slave."

"No, she's not. I know her too. She's a free woman of color but she's a voodoo queen. All the queens are free women of color."

"But I see her in church often. She's a Catholic. How can she be a voodoo queen? I thought the voodoos worshiped snakes."

"I don't know, but a lot of voodoos are Catholic. They go to the cathedral on Sunday and to Bayou St. John on Saturday nights for their voodoo ceremonies and a lot of dancing— and other things you don't want to hear about. One of the queens is a relative of ours, Marie Laveau."

"Yes, I know; she's the one that even Americans go to for their gris-gris charms. Maman says she's a wonderful hairdresser."

All the while, Antoinette and little Samuel had their faces pressed to the fence, their eyes glued to the voodoo queen, watching every twist and turn as she danced with her snake. Antoinette was tapping her feet and Samuel was nodding his head up and down and softly clapping his hands.

"It looks to me like they're enjoying the show," said Uncle Félix, pointing to the children. "This is a lot of fun for them."

After a time the drumbeats stopped and the dance came to an abrupt halt. Some of the slaves gathered around the voodoo queen, laughing and talking, ignoring the onlookers. One of them jumped atop a cannon in the middle of the square and performed a series of acrobatic tricks, finally somersaulting back to the ground. His companions clapped and shouted in admiration.

"I wish I could do that," said Samuel.

"Why do they have a cannon here in the square?" asked

Antoinette. "I thought they were only in the Place d'Armes, where the soldiers march up and down."

"You know that cannon you hear every night at nine o'clock to warn the slaves to get home? Well, that's the cannon."

"And I guess we'd better get home," said Henriette. "Cécile will be looking for us."

As they turned to go, Uncle Félix asked her, "What did you think of the dancing and chanting? There really wasn't any voodoo that I could tell—only the snake dance—but no casting spells or trances or anything like that, just everyone having a good time."

"Yes, you're right," Henriette replied. After a moment she added, "But it's too bad that Sunday's the only day they're allowed to have a good time. And what about those 'Kaintucks,' the flatboatmen, making fun of them? Do you think they noticed?"

"They're too busy enjoying themselves dancing the bamboula and singing to notice those ignorant Americans from the wilds of Kentucky. Anyway, the slaves don't pay any attention to them. They know what they are."

Uncle Félix escorted them home and, before bidding them good-bye, looked solemnly at Henriette. "Dear Henriette, you know I've been close to you since you were a little girl, even younger than Antoinette. I know you want to do good works, but don't forget your family. People are talking about you and your friends spending too much time with slaves."

Henriette started to say something but stopped.

"You're a beautiful young woman; we hoped you would settle down with someone and have a family, like Cécile."

Henriette shook her head, paused a moment, then firmly declared: "But I'm not like Cécile, *mon oncle,* and I don't want the kind of life she has. Oh, I wish you could understand. So many people are suffering and I know God wants me to help them. It's . . ."

Uncle Félix interrupted. "I see now. You don't have to explain. If that's the life you really want, well, I won't say any more. But remember, whatever you do and whatever people say, your Oncle Félix will always be here for you."

Henriette flung her arms around him and said, as she had said many times during her childhood, "*Ah, cher Oncle Félix, you are wonderful!*" He laughed and gave the children a kiss, turned, and waved as he walked away.

Henriette took Antoinette and Samuel into the house and delivered them into the welcoming arms of Nanou, then ran off to meet her friends at St. Mary's Chapel. It was a relief to enter the quiet of St. Mary's. She knelt at the altar rail and prayed for all the slaves she had seen at Congo Square. She also prayed for Uncle Félix and the rest of her family, hoping that they might better understand her mission.

The silence of the sanctuary was suddenly broken by the sound of footsteps and Henriette smiled, knowing they belonged to her friends. She turned and saw that Marie-Jeanne was with them. They were surprised when Henriette told them where she had spent the afternoon.

"My *maman* doesn't like me going to Congo Square," said Joséphine.

"Why not?" asked Marie-Jeanne.

"She thinks there's too much voodoo."

"You know, I didn't see much voodoo," replied Henriette, "just one of the voodoo queens dancing with a snake. They were having such a good time. It reminded me a little bit of Mardi Gras."

"Well, this year's Mardi Gras was pretty wild," said Juliette. "The *Courrier* had an article about how destructive some of the maskers were, throwing mud and even stones at people's houses."

"Yes, I remember," said Henriette. "I guess a lot of people use Carnival time as an excuse for drinking too much and carousing."

"That happens in France too," said Marie-Jeanne with a wry smile.

Joséphine chimed in. "Remember a few years ago it got so bad that they wouldn't let people mask at all during Mardi Gras."

Henriette smiled. "Well, let's hope that doesn't happen again. Mardi Gras is like Sunday at Congo Square. It gives people a chance to forget their cares for a while and have a little joy in their lives."

They were silent for a few moments until Joséphine said softly, "One of my greatest joys is being with all of you. But my *maman* makes it so hard for me. She's always telling me I spend too much time with you helping slaves when I should be helping her."

"Well, she's not alone in that," retorted Juliette. She turned to Marie-Jeanne. "Many people in our Creole community disapprove of our work with the slaves."

"I've sensed that," said Marie-Jeanne. "But don't let that stop you. You're doing God's work."

"They notice other things we do too. They don't like us being baptismal sponsors for slave women's babies or going to the potter's field with them when one of their loved ones dies. The hardest thing, I think, is burying the slaves who die alone in the street. Once we had to dig the grave ourselves."

"*Oh, mon Dieu!*" exclaimed Marie-Jeanne, clutching her breast.

"Of course our families don't know about that," said Henriette. "As it is, sometimes people jeer at us when they see us coming from the potter's field." She paused a moment. "But for me, the most upsetting thing is my sister, Cécile. She tells me everyday I'm too obsessed with the needs of slaves."

Henriette was remembering just a few days before when Cécile told her in an exasperated tone, "Henriette, you're twenty-two years old now. Don't you think it's time for you to look to your future? You can't spend the rest of your life taking care of slaves. You have to take care of yourself too."

Cécile's words remained with Henriette as the girls and Marie-Jeanne left St. Mary's and went their separate ways. Henriette's steps were slow as she recalled her rebuttal to her sister. Did it truly express her feelings about her vocation?

"I know how you feel, Cécile," she had told her. "But what I really want is to serve God in a religious community. I've told you that. And since I can't, then I must serve him in the only other way I can."

Those words certainly did not convince her sister. Henriette almost smiled as she remembered Cécile's reaction, throwing up her hands in exasperation and almost shouting, "What do you mean? The only other way you can? You could be thinking of settling down like I did and having a family of your own to care for instead of ignorant slaves." But then, seeing Henriette's stricken face, she took pity on her sister and hugged her, saying, "Whatever you do, I want you to be happy."

Henriette mulled over her sister's final words. They were a consolation, but for days afterward she herself wondered if her vocation were truly from God. One day at prayer, again in St. Mary's Chapel, she received an unmistakable confirmation. In the midst of her confusion, she appealed to God for guidance. Kneeling quietly and gazing on the crucified Christ, she suddenly felt a stabbing thrill of joy throughout her whole being. Tears came to her eyes and she rested in that joy for she did not know how long. But when awareness of her surroundings returned, she knew beyond a shadow of a doubt that God wanted her to found a community of women dedicated to serving the poor, the elderly, and especially his most neglected ones, the slaves. Words suddenly flooded her consciousness and she repeated over and over, "I believe in God. I hope in God. I love. I wish to live and die for God." It was to be her mantra for the rest of her life.

For some time Henriette kept all these things in her heart, but one day she spoke tentatively to Marie-Jeanne about her desire to organize a group of women dedicated to teaching slaves and caring for the sick and elderly.

Marie-Jeanne's eyes grew wide with excitement. "Oh, if only you could!" she exclaimed and quickly added, "I want to help you."

Henriette was encouraged by Marie-Jeanne's reaction

and the next day shared this news with Juliette, who was equally delighted.

"How wonderful!" Juliette exclaimed. "With Marie-Jeanne to help, I'm sure you can do it. And, of course, you have me and Joséphine with you all the way." Henriette smiled. It was not often that Juliette displayed such exuberance.

For several weeks the four women spoke of practically nothing else but how to go about forming a group and how to define the mission and support it once they got it organized. Henriette, however, was a bit concerned that Joséphine might not be able to follow through on her desire to be part of their community.

"We know she wants to join us, but her family is against it," she confided to Juliette. "They're still determined that she'll marry. Goodness knows she has enough suitors. At least they've accepted the fact that she'll never agree to an alliance with a white man."

"But Joséphine insists she doesn't want to marry at all, just like us," said Juliette.

In fact, Joséphine was so enthusiastic about Henriette's plan that she set about immediately spreading the word among the young women of her neighborhood. Some of them showed interest in joining them. Prompted by the prospect of success, Henriette decided that it was time to test her idea with Archbishop Blanc, who had on more than one occasion expressed his gratitude to Henriette and Juliette for their good works. One day she saw the archbishop walking slowly toward his residence with head bowed after a meeting with the cathedral trustees. Henriette knew he was sorely taxed by their ideological and obstinate behavior and their frequent refusals to accept the appointments he made. It often seemed that they were working against him instead of with him.

When he saw Henriette, the frown left his face and he smiled. "Ah, Henriette, you are a bright spot in my day. How are things going with you and Juliette?" Henriette smiled and seized this opportunity to ask for an appointment to see him about "an important matter." He lifted his eyebrows in speculation but did not ask what the important matter was, just told her to come see him the next morning.

Henriette could hardly get to sleep that night and was at the archbishop's office for nine o'clock. "*Bonjour,* Mlle Henriette," Louise, the housekeeper, greeted her with a smile and showed her to the archbishop's office.

"Well, Henriette," said Archbishop Blanc, "it's not often that I have such a welcome visitor." He motioned her to a chair. "So, what's this 'important matter' you wish to see me about?"

He listened attentively as Henriette told of her dream of formally organizing a group of women to serve the needs of the poor, the elderly, and especially the slaves. "What do you think, Excellency?" she asked.

He paused a moment, then smiled. "Of course, you're already doing the things such a society would do, Henriette, and thank God for that. But I like your idea. This ungodly town needs more women like you. You know what my visitors from France call it?" Henriette shook her head. "Babylon. That's how they describe this New Orleans of ours, a pagan city full of sin and vice. A lawless river town, that's what it is." He shook his head and frowned. But looking up at Henriette, he smiled and said, "I think you're right in wanting to organize your mission, especially if you now have others to join you. You have my blessing. Now, what can I do to help?"

"Oh, having your blessing, Excellency, is a wonderful beginning—we're so grateful." Henriette was almost in tears she was so affected at the archbishop's enthusiastic response.

Archbishop Blanc paused a moment, then looking intently at Henriette, he said, "I have heard that you had hoped to join a religious order and serve our Lord as a nun, Henriette. Though you have been disappointed in that, perhaps this is what God wants of you at this time. Perhaps it's where he needs you."

Henriette looked down and thought a moment. "Yes," she murmured. "I think it is."

"Now, what's your next step?"

"As I said, we have a number of women who want to join us, so we'll need to decide on some basic rules and describe our mission more fully."

The archbishop nodded his head. "That would be a good beginning. And when you have your plans put together, come see me again. Meanwhile, this is the best news I've had in a long time. May God be with you."

Henriette could hardly wait to tell the others. They were overjoyed and wanted to waste no time in formally organizing their society. They gathered their companions together and under Henriette's leadership adopted rules and goals: to minister to the elderly, the sick, and the dying and to teach the truths of their faith to slaves and people of color and prepare them to receive the sacraments. They also emphasized their own need to live lives beyond reproach and to be models of compassion and edifying behavior. They agreed to pay monthly dues, which would be used for their mission.

"We should have a motto," Henriette told them, "something we can identify with our mission. What shall it be?"

Juliette frowned. Joséphine raised her eyebrows and folded her arms in thought. "I have an idea," she said after a few moments. "I read once that the earliest Christians had a motto, just like you're talking about. I think it was . . . ," she paused and wrinkled her brow. "That was it: one heart and one soul. How does that sound?"

"One heart and one soul," repeated Henriette thoughtfully, her head tilted to one side. She looked around at the group. "I like it. What do you think, Juliette?"

"It's perfect," declared Juliette. "What better model could we have than Jesus' earliest followers? That's what we'll be— one heart and one soul."

It was agreed. And so on that day, November 21, 1836, the Feast of the Presentation of Our Lady in the Temple, they formally established a society, calling it the Congregation of the Sisters of the Presentation of Our Lady. Henriette was elected their leader.

"Do you think we can really call ourselves 'sisters'?" timidly asked one of the group. "We're not real sisters, like the Ursulines."

"Well, no, we aren't," said Henriette with a winsome smile, "but one of these days, if it's God's will, we might be real sisters." Enthusiasm was high and all the members felt the strength that mutual support gave them. Henriette knew they would need all the tenacity they could get; it was not long before the new members of their group discovered that their families and friends looked with suspicion or outright antipathy toward their mission—despite the archbishop's approbation. As expected, Joséphine's family was especially antagonistic, for they still had high hopes that she would marry. "What do you mean by calling yourselves 'sisters'?" her mother asked indignantly. "They're not your sisters and it's not like you're a nun."

Joséphine continued her work as a seamstress but usually managed to get away for an hour of prayer with the other members of the society at St. Mary's Chapel. She faithfully attended their meetings and was a caring attendant at many an elderly slave's sickbed and a consoling presence at their funerals.

Cécile had finally reconciled herself to Henriette's commitment to her mission. She still counted on her help with the children and the running of family affairs since their mother was now too mentally and emotionally disabled to help at all. But Cécile did not begrudge Henriette the time she spent with the society's mission and no longer nagged her about getting married.

The greatest support Henriette and her followers had was from Archbishop Blanc. However, there soon arrived in New Orleans one who would be their staunchest champion of all.

Chapter 10

Saving Grace

1837

One day in September as Henriette was heading to the French Market, she was stopped in her tracks by an amusing spectacle on the opposite side of the street. She muffled a giggle at the sight of an unfamiliar figure, a priest, she assumed from his garb, trying to decide how to cross the muddy roadway. Several times he lifted his cassock and put a foot out, then pulled it back, looking around for some solution to his problem. When he saw Henriette he looked sheepishly at her and greeted her with a faint smile. *"Bonjour, mademoiselle,* I'm new to your city and trying to figure out how to get around."

Henriette smiled back and lifted her own skirt a trifle to show him the rim of mud around the bottom as well as her mud-caked shoes. She shook her head and said, "I think the only way is to plunge in and get across as fast as you can. The city says it's going to put in new brick roadways, but who knows when?"

She watched as he resolutely put one foot into the muddy road, then the other, and was soon at her side. The bottom of his cassock looked just like the hem of Henriette's skirt. "I'm Father Rousselon," he said. "Archbishop Blanc's new assistant. I'm from Lyon, where the streets are all bricked, and I must say, I miss them."

Henriette smiled. "The archbishop told me he was

getting a new assistant. Welcome to our city, Father. I'm Henriette Delille."

Father Rousselon raised his eyebrows. "Ah, Henriette Delille, the archbishop told me all about you and your friends who do so much good in the city. I'm delighted to meet you."

A carriage rumbled by, causing Henriette and Father Rousselon to move farther away from the gutters to avoid getting splashed. "I guess I'll get used to this," said Father with a rueful smile. "I didn't realize New Orleans was such a rustic city. Oh . . . of course, I know it's very sophisticated in many ways, with opera and theatre and elaborate balls—and fine cuisine."

"Well, Father, don't be surprised if one day you come across a dead dog or even a goat in the middle of the roadway. That still happens but not as much as it used to."

Several days later, Henriette met Father Rousselon again, this time at St. Claude School, where she was teaching a First Communion class. As he approached the classroom he heard her say, "Always remember, children, that Jesus loves you no matter who you are or where you live or whether you're rich or poor. He loves you so much he died for you—and for me."

Father poked his head in the door and smiled at Henriette and the children. "Mlle Delille is absolutely right."

"Father Rousselon," said Henriette. "Children, this is our new priest at the cathedral. Stand up and perhaps he will give us a blessing."

They immediately jumped to their feet and Father raised his hand, making the sign of the cross and saying in Latin, "I bless all of you, in the name of the Father and of the Son and of the Holy Spirit."

"May I see you after the class is over, Father?" asked Henriette.

"Yes, of course. I'll be down the hall preparing the confirmation class."

When her charges were dismissed, Henriette found Father Rousselon and asked if he would come to the next society gathering to meet the members, lead them in prayer, and perhaps give a talk on some spiritual subject of his choosing. He said he would be more than happy to do that.

However, before that time came, he received an urgent request at the bishop's residence to come to the bedside of a dying woman. The dour young sacristan who gave him the message said, "One of them Presentation women wants you, Father. I wouldn't go if I was you. It's probably some old slave that those women are always making a fuss over. She's down the Quarter in some stinky old barn."

Father Rousselon looked at him in disdain, shook his head, then grabbed his case and quickly went to meet the messenger, a young quadroon woman he had not seen before.

"Thank you so much, Father. Henriette said you would come. I'm Joséphine Charles. It's old Celestine; she's really in a bad way. She's been sick for months, but we think this is the end for her. She's always calling for a priest, but this is the first time . . ." Joséphine paused, looked confused, and quickly added, "Just follow me, please."

She hurriedly led him through the streets and across Esplanade Avenue to an alley at the end of which stood a ramshackle stable. It was getting dark and if Joséphine had not had a lantern Father would have stumbled and fallen several times as they found their way to a crude lean-to attached to the stable. They entered to find Henriette hovering over a pallet on which lay an elderly, shriveled-looking black woman, her breath coming in raspy fits and starts.

Henriette jumped up. "Oh, Father," she whispered. "Thank you so much for coming; I knew you would. Celestine was so afraid she would die without the last rites. And I think you're just in time."

She turned and knelt again close to Celestine, taking her hand and gently stroking her brow. "Father Rousselon is here, Celestine. Your prayers are answered," she whispered into the old woman's ear. "You can go to our heavenly Father in peace."

Father quickly took out his handkerchief and coughed because of the putrid smell of the place. He wondered at Henriette's and Joséphine's fortitude in the oppressive, foul-smelling shack. "I'm glad I was able to get here in time," he whispered. "Are you sure she's that bad off?"

When Henriette nodded yes, he opened his case and took out the holy oils. Just then Juliette arrived with Marie-Jeanne. They all knelt as Father anointed Celestine and recited the prayers for the dying. Celestine's eyes fluttered open several times and she tried to raise her head when Father bent down close to her, but the effort was too much. Juliette said she would spend the night and let the others know how Celestine was doing in the morning.

As Henriette, Joséphine, and Father walked out, Father turned to them, frowning, and asked, "Why is she in this awful place? Who are her owners? Why aren't they taking care of her?"

Henriette looked puzzled for a moment. This was not unusual in New Orleans. She had tended many abandoned slaves. As she hesitated, Father persisted, "I assume she's a slave and belongs to someone?"

"Yes, Father, you're right," Henriette replied, "but when Celestine got sick some months ago and wasn't able to work, her owners just put her out to beg in the street. She took shelter in this little place by the stable and has been here ever since."

Father shook his head. It seemed too incredible a thing for him to grasp. "How is that possible?" he wondered aloud.

They walked sadly and in silence to the cathedral rectory. Father's parting words remained with Henriette for a long time, "We have much to pray for in this city of yours, Henriette."

* * *

In the following years, Father Rousselon often called on Henriette when administering the sacraments. At times she served as sponsor for baptism or marriage. This was especially true when legal sanctions such as fines and imprisonment required his discretion.

One Thursday morning, as Henriette wended her way

toward St. Mary's for just such an occasion, she was thinking how much her life had changed in recent years. It was now 1841; Cécile's children were grown. Antoinette, Cécile's oldest child, now in her late teens, had married M. Etienne Darse, a well-established free man of color. It was comforting for Henriette to know that her niece was protected by the legal status of matrimony that Cécile had never enjoyed. She recalled the bitter court battles after M. Hart's death when Cécile, whom everyone thought well provided for, was suddenly faced with the threat of penury.

"Why would his brothers not acknowledge M. Hart's own children?" Cécile had tearfully asked the lawyer. "His will clearly states that the children were to inherit one-fifth of the property after his death."

"M. Hart's brothers filed another will that contradicts yours," explained the lawyer, Mr. John Slidell. "The courts will settle the affair but it may take time. I'll do my best to see that you and your children are provided for," he promised.

Two years of legal wrangling followed before John Slidell was able to win a suitable inheritance for Cécile and her children. In the meantime, Cécile's health had visibly deteriorated under the stress of the prolonged court battle.

As Henriette was approaching St. Mary's, she crossed paths with Annie, a young slave for whom she had been a baptismal sponsor years before.

"Bonjour, marraine," said Annie, smiling broadly at her godmother. "You goin' sponsorin' again?"

"Annie, how nice to see you. Yes, Father Rousselon sent word, so I'm on my way to meet him."

"You and your ladies helps Father Rousselon in lots a ways," Annie volunteered. "He say you be helpin' him do God's work."

"Father Rousselon is very kind. The truth is, Annie, he helps us too. We find the lost sheep, but he brings them the sacraments."

"He say you specially help ol' 'bandon' slaves. Used to be some ol' slaves just die in the street. Everybody know that ain't right, but nobody come to help 'em die better.'"

Henriette smiled at her godchild but before she could answer, they heard a high-pitched woman's voice calling out, "*Au secours!* Help! Stop him. Please, stop him!"

Seeing no one nearby, she and Annie ran to the corner where, in the middle of the block, their eyes locked on a terrible sight. A snarling black dog, standing on its hind legs, had a woman pinned against a wrought-iron fence. The man holding the dog's leash, laughing and hurling insults, made no attempt to stop the attack. Drawing close to the frightened woman who was spilling the contents of her basket, Henriette realized it was Jocelyn, one of the sisters. She also recognized the attacker screaming at her, "This ought a teach you to keep to your own kind."

Henriette was so enraged she couldn't help shouting, "M. de Villiers, call off your dog at once. What is the meaning of this?"

Glowering, the man yanked on the dog's leash and turned to face the person calling him by name. "Ah, so it's you, Henriette Delille. You're the one who started all this! The very idea of getting our free people of color to mix and meddle with the lower classes."

"M. de Villiers, how can you call yourself a Christian and talk like that?" she challenged, putting her arm around Jocelyn to steady her as they backed away from the growling dog.

"Down, Bruno!" the man yelled. Then, again looking at Henriette, "Bad enough you were pokin' around in those squalid neighborhoods by yourself, but then you had to get a whole passel of women doin' your 'holier than thou' activities. Have you no shame?"

"Shame?" Henriette stood to her full height and almost chuckled as she retorted, "Hah! I'm looking at a big man with a big dog who attacks a solitary woman on an errand of mercy. Shame, you say? I'm afraid the shame is on you, M. de Villiers."

At this, the man turned crimson and glared at Henriette. "You're a disgrace to all of us. Everyone knows your family has tried to curb your excesses but apparently to no avail."

Realizing that nothing could be achieved by a continued

exchange of angry words, Henriette stepped back, taking Jocelyn with her. "Excuse me, M. de Villiers, I must care for my friend. As you can see, her clothes are muddy and torn and she's had a terrifying experience."

M. de Villiers turned on his heel and left, pulling the growling Bruno behind him.

Half a block away Annie had watched the whole episode, too terrified to approach. She now ran to the two women, crying, "Oh, Mlle Henriette. What a terrible thing to happen. What can I do to help?"

"Annie, could you take Jocelyn home? Father Rousselon is still waiting for me at St. Mary's."

"Oh, yes ma'am. But weren't you afeared o' that big dog? He could'a attacked you too."

"Normally, I would have been afraid, Annie. But I was very angry and wanted to help Jocelyn. Perhaps it was grace that did the rest."

Poor Jocelyn, still sobbing more from fright than from injury, tried to catch her breath as Henriette handed her into Annie's care and assured her she would come by to check on her as soon as she could.

"I'll take you home, Mlle Jocelyn. You goin' be a'right," said Annie as she led the still-shaking woman down the block.

Henriette, realizing it was getting late, hurried to the church. Father Rousselon was in the vestibule speaking to a young free woman of color and a white man, two people Henriette had never seen. Father smiled and beckoned to her. "*Bonjour,* Henriette. I'd like you to meet Madeleine Hébert and Rémy Duroc. They are here to be married. You understand that we couldn't announce the banns publicly. I'd like you to witness their union."

"Yes, Father, I'm happy to do that." Henriette shook hands with them and smiled broadly. "This is a very special day for you. I wish you both much happiness."

"And here comes the sacristan, Olivier Bournois. He'll be the other witness," said Father. "After the ceremony, we'll go into the sacristy to sign papers. Legal issues prevent us from entering them in the parish archives."

"We understand, Father," said Rémy, "but we want to be married by a priest. Very soon we plan to live in my hometown back in France."

"Which town do you come from?" asked Father.

"I come from Pau at the foot of the Pyrénées Mountains," Rémy answered.

"It's a very beautiful area," Father remarked. "Madeleine will have a good life there though different from her life here in New Orleans. What will you do back in Pau?"

"My parents have a small sheep farm in the foothills outside the city. Papa takes care of the farming with my older brother, and my mother has a cottage industry making goat cheese. My parents are getting old so my brother and I will run the farm and Madeleine will learn to make goat cheese."

"Sounds like your future is well secured," said Father.

No one but the witnesses was in attendance at the simple ceremony. Though it was illegal for people of mixed races to marry, Father Rousselon said it was a bad law so he paid no attention to it. He had to be discreet, however, in order to avoid legal problems. The papers to be signed were hidden in a secret place.

After the ceremony, he invited them all to the rectory for a small celebration with a glass of champagne to toast the newlyweds. Madeleine had never tasted champagne and laughed because she said it tickled her nose. Henriette enjoyed the feeling of lightness she got from the bubbles, and Rémy remarked on what a fine vintage it was.

After the couple left, Father Rousselon chatted with Henriette for a short time. "How's your sister's health?" he inquired.

"I'm afraid she's not at all well. The doctors don't seem to know what's wrong. She has trouble breathing. She also looks bad and feels tired all the time," replied Henriette.

"Please let me know if there's anything I can do. And what of the society?" he inquired, changing the subject.

At this point Henriette relayed to him the incident of Jocelyn's being mauled by M. de Villier's dog.

"Was she hurt?" he asked.

"The dog didn't bite her but she was still trembling from fear when I left her with Annie. Now she'll probably be afraid to walk down the street," said Henriette.

"I hear there have been other such incidents. Perhaps it would be best if in future two members would go out together," advised Father Rousselon.

"Yes, I've already decided to do that, Father." She paused, then added, "It's bad enough to endure insults from strangers, but when our own family and friends ridicule us and try to harm us, it's heartbreaking."

He shook his head in disbelief. Then, in an effort to raise Henriette's spirits, he said, "Remember, Henriette, Jesus himself often endured ridicule from those who didn't understand him or his work."

"You're right, Father, and at least so far no one has tried to stone us. I'll remind the others of that." Then, noting the late hour, she added, "I'd better get home now."

When Henriette arrived at her sister's house, she was alarmed to find her nieces and nephews sitting in the parlor with Pouponne, all hushed and looking frightened. She thought immediately of Cécile and asked, "What's the matter?"

"It's Maman," said Antoinette. "She was feeling very bad this morning and couldn't breathe. Then she fainted. The doctor's with her now."

"My poor Cécile," cried Henriette. "How long has the doctor been with her?"

"About a half-hour," said Antoinette. "Nanou was so frightened when Maman fainted that she sent for me, and I sent for Dr. Briand."

Just then Nanou, who had been with the doctor, came into the room in tears. "Oh, Miss Henriette, it's bad. The doctor say it's very bad."

"What do you mean, Nanou? Did he say why it's bad?" questioned Henriette, trying to remain calm.

"Yes'm. Doctor say she ain't gonna make it dis time," said Nanou, trying to stifle her sobs.

A door opened and Dr. Briand appeared, looking worn

and serious. "I'm afraid her heart is failing," he said, shaking his head. "You may all go in to see her, but I don't think she'll regain consciousness."

Pouponne began weeping uncontrollably as she and Cécile's four children followed Henriette into the bedroom to gather around the big four-poster bed. Cécile was pale and lying very still. From time to time little rattling noises emanated from her throat as she tried to breathe.

Henriette beckoned to Nanou and said, "You must pull yourself together, Nanou. Go find Father Rousselon and ask him to come immediately. Tell him Cécile is dying."

"Yes'm," Nanou choked out between her sobs.

Putting her arm around Pouponne, Henriette gently led her to the bedside, then took out her rosary as a signal for all to kneel. They responded as she led them in praying the Sorrowful Mysteries. By the time they had finished, they heard Nanou ushering Father Rousselon into the house.

"Father, thank you for coming," said Henriette, rising to greet him. "Will you give Cécile the last rites?"

"Yes, I have the sacred oils with me." Father Rousselon then proceeded to lead the group in prayers for the dying as he anointed Cécile's body.

"She seems to be resting more easily," said Dr. Briand, who as a longtime friend had remained with the family. "This often results from receiving the holy viaticum."

They saw Cécile's eyelids flutter slightly as she tried to focus on the scene surrounding her bed. When she saw Henriette, she feebly extended her hand, which Henriette grasped lovingly in both of hers. "Henriette, you are so good. Pray for me," she whispered, smiling weakly at her mother, then at each of her children in turn. Having no strength left, she closed her eyes. Henriette, whose hands were still holding onto Cécile's, felt her fingers relax. Not a sound was heard from the bed, not even breathing.

After several minutes Dr. Briand said softly, "She's gone." For a long moment, there was silence. Then Pouponne let out a heartbreaking sob followed by the sound of others dissolving into tears.

Mourning shrouded the house in sadness. The loving hands of Nanou and Betsy prepared Cécile's body under Henriette's supervision and for the last time, as in days gone by, it was Pouponne who chose her daughter's clothing. Late the following afternoon, Jean arrived from St. Martinville, having received word by telegraph of his sister's passing. Upon entering the parlor, he was overcome at the sight of his vivacious younger sister lying lifeless. In a flash, he keenly remembered her sixteenth birthday, her joyful eagerness to attend the balls, her alliance with M. Hart, and finally, the births of her four children. He had loved Cécile's enthusiasm and her willingness to accept life as she found it. She had even come to approve of Henriette's digression from family tradition and social customs—something he himself was unable to condone.

Two days after Cécile's passing, Father Rousselon conducted a beautiful but somber funeral service at the Mortuary Chapel. Family members, including aunts, uncles, and cousins plus countless friends, gathered to bid farewell to Cécile and to mourn her passing. Many of these same people remembered gathering in the cathedral to celebrate Cécile's baptism by Père Antoine.

Henriette in particular was shocked that her sister had died at the young age of thirty-four. The two had grown much closer over the last year. Together they had weathered the storms of Pouponne's drawn-out illnesses and legal problems. Then there was M. Hart's death and the court battles over his will. Cécile had been grateful to Henriette for her support throughout these ordeals and especially for having helped to raise her four children. She had become more tolerant of Henriette's determination to follow her own life's path, realizing that her sister was called to do something special.

In the days and months following the funeral, Henriette attended daily mass at the cathedral to pray for her family and to ask God's guidance. She knew that the Congregation of the Sisters of the Presentation was only the beginning of her mission. She began to envision a group of women of color living together, bound by vows to a life of ministry, and with papal approval. They would then be a true religious community "of one heart and one soul." Innumerable obstacles related to Cécile's will and providing for her children kept Henriette from immediately realizing her dream. Still, she sensed that the path before her was beginning to clear. As painful as the death of Cécile was, it would ultimately open a door to greater independence.

These thoughts ran through her mind as she left the cathedral one morning in October. When she stepped into Père Antoine Alley opposite the Presbytère, she was greeted by Louise, Archbishop Blanc's housekeeper.

"Bonjour, Mlle Henriette. The bishop's wantin' to see you. He be's in his study."

"Do you mean right now, Louise?"

"Yes'm, right now be good."

Within minutes Henriette was ushered into Archbishop Blanc's office. He rose to greet her as she entered. *"Bonjour,* Henriette. As always, I'm glad to see you. Please come in and have a seat," he said, indicating a chair opposite his desk. "Louise, would you be good enough to bring us some *café au lait* and some of those delicious beignets you made this morning—if there are any left?"

"Sho'nuf, Excellency. I be's bringin' a tray right away," she said, beaming.

"Now, Henriette, I want you to tell me how things are going with the Congregation. Father Rousselon tells me that in spite of losing a few members, your work continues. Still, you must get discouraged from time to time."

"Your Excellency, as long as our Lord gives us his grace, we'll continue to do his work. That's our mission."

"How many members do you have now?"

"We're fourteen at present, with both married and single ladies as members," replied Henriette.

"I understand that your members help anyone in need, regardless of social standing or legal sanctions."

"That's true, your Excellency."

"Henriette, since your society does so much good work for the Church and is dedicated to our Lady, I've written to Rome requesting that your group be joined to the Roman College of Sodalities of Our Lady. They have answered my letter saying that you are to be affiliated under the title of the Annunciation of Our Lady."

Henriette looked puzzled. "I'm not sure I understand what that means, your Excellency."

"It means that the prayers and works of your members are united to members of the Church all over the world. The women of your society, although they cannot be considered nuns, will receive many graces and spiritual benefits."

"Oh, your Excellency, thank you. Wait till I tell our members! They'll be so happy," said Henriette, deeply moved.

"In addition, Henriette, I think we should make a public announcement. Why don't you all attend the nine o'clock mass here at the cathedral next Sunday? After the sermon, I will publicly confer the charter on the Sisters of the Presentation," said the archbishop, looking very pleased. "Your work in the city will be easier if people know you have the approval of your bishop as well as acknowledgment in Rome."

"Oh, that would be wonderful, your Excellency," said Henriette meeting his gaze, her eyes filled with joyful gratitude.

There was a slight knock at the door and Louise entered bearing a tray of *café au lait* and beignets.

"You know, Henriette, since coming to New Orleans, I've grown accustomed to the wonderful food here, and I especially enjoy drinking this delicious coffee." Louise said nothing but left the room chuckling to herself, pleased that her cooking was appreciated.

When Henriette left the bishop, it was with a heart filled with joy and gratitude. She dashed back across the alley into the cathedral. To think that people in Rome knew and approved of her little group was an unexpected milestone in the journey toward her goal.

Chapter 11

On the Move

After Cécile's funeral, Henriette, who was in charge of settling her sister's affairs, sent for Jean, asking him to help her. He agreed to return to the city and stay until Cécile's three youngest children were placed with relatives and the former house on Burgundy Street could be prepared for his mother.

"Thank heaven you still have connections in real estate, Jean, and that you know contractors who can refurbish the old house. It'll be a fine dwelling for Maman and Nanou," said Henriette.

"And for you too," he replied, looking askance.

"Yes, but I'll stay only till I find a home for our society. Then I'll live with them."

"Do you mean to tell me you're going to continue this foolishness of yours when your own mother needs your care?"

"But Jean," she replied, "Nanou will take care of Maman better than anyone, just as she always has."

"That may be so, but Nanou's getting old too and she could get sick any day."

"Nanou is in excellent health, Jean, and if anything should happen to her, of course I would take care of Maman. Besides, Maman's physical health is not in any danger. It's just that when she gets her headaches and dizzy spells she does outlandish things."

"Exactly! Like trying to negotiate false business deals."

"Jean, that happened only twice and both times the lawyer

131

contacted me immediately to verify the circumstances. No harm was ever done."

"Harm? You see no harm in letting our mother roam about the streets so outsiders can see how irrational she is? Henriette, have you no family pride at all?"

"You mean, do I care about what people think? No, not as long as I know I'm doing the right thing."

"Henriette, you're unreasonable! Why have we never convinced you that the right thing, the sensible thing, was to stick with our family traditions?"

"By sensible, I suppose you mean become someone's concubine, right?"

"You make it sound so sordid. All any of us ever wanted was to have a better life."

"And what about the slaves, Jean? Who makes life better for them?"

"Why does it have to be you, Henriette?"

"Because I believe it's what God wants me to do."

"How do you know what God wants?"

"I know, Jean. It's like a voice within me that I can't ignore."

"My, my, voices! I suppose next you'll tell me you're having visions. You must think you're some kind of Jeanne d'Arc? And your mission is to save the slaves?

"I know I can't save all of them, but if I can help even a few, it's worth doing. Jean, surely you realize that somewhere in the past we're all related to people from Africa. They're family too."

"That's exactly what I am trying to forget, Henriette. Why do you think I moved out of New Orleans? Because your 'good deeds' label me."

"Yes, I know that by living away you can pass for white. But, Jean, why run away from the truth?"

"There's no talking reason to you. The truth is, you're the one running away from our family. You are stubborn, Henriette, and you're turning your back on your own mother."

Henriette turned from him and moved toward the window

so he would not see how deeply his words cut her. She loved her family and never intended to turn her back on them. It was true she often went her own way, but Nanou was there to take care of them and Pouponne preferred Cécile's company. But Cécile was not there now and Nanou was getting older. Was she turning her back on them? Was she pursuing God's will or just following her own headstrong ideas? She turned to face her brother.

"Jean, do you pray?"

He stiffened as he answered, "If you must know, I make my Easter duty. And all my children have been baptized."

"But do you pray, Jean? Do you ask God to help you know his will?"

Jean glared at his sister, resentment in his eyes, then turned and left the room. Henriette took a deep breath, knowing the truth without his having answered. She decided to let events take their own course until she could see her way clearly, both with her family and her society.

Not long after Cécile's death, Henriette moved her mother along with Nanou and Betsy into their house on Burgundy Street. She moved in with them. Just when she thought she had settled her family matters and was free to make plans for uniting the society under one roof, Amelia, one of Cécile's children, died unexpectedly, causing more pain to the diminishing family. Henriette grieved with the others yet this time her heart remained at peace. These seeming setbacks were also part of God's plan. She needed simply to embrace them as his will. Take one day at a time, that was her path.

Henriette's trust was confirmed in the spring when another serious yellow fever epidemic struck the city. Countless victims and their families turned to Henriette and her followers for nursing care. She was thankful to be at home. God had arranged for to her to remain with her mother and still care for the yellow jack victims. The rest would come in due time.

The fever was pernicious and though the sisters were spared from falling victim to the plague, they did not spare themselves. They rose early and often worked past midnight bringing comfort and care to whoever needed help. At times they found themselves nursing the very people who had insulted them.

Late one afternoon, Juliette was asked to come to a Creole cottage on Dumaine Street to care for the man of the house. He had gone to work that morning feeling fine but was suddenly taken ill and brought home with a raging fever.

"Oh, Sister, I can't thank you enough for coming," said his wife, beside herself with worry. "By the time they brought him home the fever was so high all of his clothes were drenched in perspiration."

When Juliette looked at the crumpled heap lying on the bed, she gasped and put her hands to her heart. Suddenly, anger welled up within her as she recognized M. de Villiers, the very man who had threatened Jocelyn with his barking dog, pinning her against a fence.

"You ladies know exactly what to do when the plague hits," said Mme de Villiers, dabbing tears from her eyes. "Even the doctors say so." It was plain she knew nothing of the incident with the dog.

Juliette breathed a quick prayer asking the Lord's help. "O dear Jesus, this man is our enemy. I know you told us we must love our enemies, but I don't know if I can." She paused for a long moment, then took a deep breath. Finally, looking at Mme de Villiers she whispered, "Please bring me a basin of warm water and as many towels as you can spare."

Together the two women spent the next hour removing the stained clothing of the half-conscious man, gently bathing him and soothing his trembling body. Then they put a clean nightshirt on him and covered him with a warm quilt.

"Keep him quiet now; he needs to sleep. When he wakes repeat the same procedure. Give him some warm broth as soon as he can swallow. You have to keep doing this till the fever breaks." Juliette spoke in a calm, reassuring voice. "What he needs most is rest and to know that you are beside him."

"Sister, you have been so kind and gentle with him. I'll try to do exactly as you did."

"If his condition worsens, send for me again," said Juliette, gathering her things. When she stepped into the street she was surprised that not a trace of anger remained in her heart. In its place she found new energy and deep peace.

When parents were stricken with the fever, the sisters took turns caring for the children. They bought groceries out of their society funds, cooked nutritious meals, and cleaned the house until the families were able to help themselves. By late fall the plague died out.

The following spring, Father Rousselon was named pastor of the newly dedicated St. Augustine Church, located on the corner of St. Claude and Bayou Road. It had been built with generous donations from Creole families, both white and black, afraid of losing their French language and culture because of the Americans flocking to the city. They were therefore delighted to have a French-speaking pastor.

Arriving at the rectory one morning, Henriette rang the bell. Father Rousselon himself answered. "Come in, Henriette. I've been waiting for you. I have some very good news," he said, a broad smile creasing his face.

"Hello, Father. Ah, can I guess? You've found a housekeeper."

"No, that's not it. Why don't you come in and sit down. Then I'll tell you what it's about." He led Henriette to the parlor and gestured toward a chair. He sat opposite her, taking his time, then finally said, "The news is not about me, but about you."

"About me?" said Henriette, cocking her head inquiringly.

"Yes, you and the sisters."

Henriette's eyes grew bright with anticipation. "And what is this good news?" she asked, trying to contain her excitement.

He paused a moment. "I've found you a house."

"A house? You mean where we can live together?" she asked, her voice rising in pitch.

"Well, yes . . . and no. But I'll explain that later," he said, piquing her curiosity. "It's a small house, but I thought it could be the beginning of something larger to come."

"Where is it? And how many of us could live there?"

"It's on St. Bernard. A few people can live there comfortably. Naturally I thought you, Juliette, and Joséphine might move in till we find a larger dwelling."

"Oh yes, Father!" Henriette rose to her feet, unable to contain her excitement. "We've often spoken of this. We need to live together. And we'll need a bigger house later on—to accept other members."

As he did not respond, Henriette began naming things they would need to set up housekeeping: beds and bedding, table and chairs, cooking utensils and table service. Father Rousselon sat back amused, letting her go on in a rush of excitement. The sound of the doorbell stopped her in mid-sentence. Still smiling, Father Rousselon did not move a muscle.

"Would you answer that for me?"

"Of course, Father," answered Henriette, glad to be helpful.

When she opened the door, there was surprise on both sides of the threshold. "Henriette!?" Juliette and Joséphine cried, pleased and a bit astonished.

"I should have guessed," laughed Henriette. "I believe Father Rousselon has been expecting you. Come in, come in."

The new arrivals guessed that something was afoot when they saw the mischievous smiles of the other two. "What's going on?" asked Juliette. "You two look like the cat that swallowed the canary."

"Why don't you tell them the good news, Henriette," said Father Rousselon.

Henriette needed no further encouragement to announce, "Father Rousselon has found us a house! We're going to live in community."

"What? Where?" they cried, hardly able to believe their ears.

Father Rousselon rose and took something from his inside pocket. "Henriette, here's the key to the house. The three of you should go over there and have a look. Come back later to tell me what you think." They hurried out, calling their thank-yous behind them.

When they returned later that afternoon, Henriette greeted him with a questioning look on her face. "Father, the house is much bigger than we thought, with room for at least six people, if not more."

"Well, what I didn't tell you this morning was that I'd like the house to serve as a shelter for some poor black women. Do you think you ladies could manage living in part of the house and sharing the other part with them? You understand, of course, they would depend on you for almost total care."

"Father, that's a wonderful idea," they agreed.

"It would be more convenient to care for them under our own roof," said Juliette.

"And where they'll be safe," added Joséphine. "Just think," she said, remembering past experiences, "they won't have to be lying on a bed of straw in some dark, foul-smelling hovel."

That very day they began planning for the move. Henriette's niece convinced her that they would help Nanou watch over Pouponne, leaving her free to pursue her dream. The following week Nanou helped them clean the house from top to bottom and Uncle Félix sent a man with a wagon to transport furniture. Though Henriette and Juliette were ready to move in, Joséphine's mother still expected her to marry. She had to stay home, at least for the time being. Even though she was disappointed, Josephine did not lose hope and came to help her friends at every opportunity.

Finally, on November 21, 1842, the Feast of the Presentation of Our Lady, Henriette and Juliette officially took up residence in their new quarters. Father Rousselon came to bless the house and Joséphine was on hand to wish them well. Gratitude filled Henriette's heart as she breathed a prayer of thanks: "Dear Lord, I feel your hand upon us. Thank you for bringing us to this house."

Just as Father brought out the holy water bottle, they heard a knock at the door. "Visitors already?" wondered Henriette as she opened the door. There stood Marie-Jeanne Aliquot with her friend and rescuer, big Samuel, the slave from the wharf. Marie-Jeanne was supporting an ill-clad, shivering woman while Samuel held another in his arms, both abandoned slaves. Having now sold St. Claude's School to the Ursulines, Marie-Jeanne continuously found ways to help slaves though she had to operate clandestinely for fear of retaliation from her neighbors. Today she brought her two latest charges to the new home where Father Rousselon had promised they would receive shelter and care.

"Come right on in," smiled Henriette, delighted at the sight of Marie-Jeanne shrouded in a hooded cloak to hide her identity.

"Gladly, dear friends. I'd like you to meet Loulie and Odette. Samuel helped me bring them to your new house. They need care badly. If you'll agree, I'd like to stay for a short time and assist you."

"Of course. You're always welcome, Marie-Jeanne. After all, you are one of us." Then she added with a chuckle, "Since you're so good at eluding the authorities while bending the law under their very noses, I think we can risk having you here for a time."

Marie-Jeanne responded with a laugh, "I keep praying to my guardian angel. He's the one who helps me slip past the vigilantes."

After Father Rousselon blessed the house and asked protection for all those within its walls, he left, along with Joséphine and Samuel.

Later that evening, when the elderly women had been fed and put to bed, Henriette, Juliette, and Marie-Jeanne sat down to reminisce over the events leading to this day. Henriette took a big breath and smiled broadly at her companions. "Do you realize what date this is?" she asked.

They were silent a moment and then Juliette smiled back and said, "Yes indeed; it's November 21, the Feast of Our Lady of the Presentation."

"That's right—the anniversary of our little society," said Henriette.

"Who would have thought back then that in six years' time we would have our very own house?" marveled Juliette.

"But don't you see? It's all providential," said Marie-Jeanne. "Our Lady has been watching over us."

"She cares for those who do her son's bidding," supplied Juliette, nodding in agreement.

"We've always asked God to guide us in helping the slaves," said Henriette. "He's been answering our prayers all along."

"That's right," said Marie-Jeanne, "and he always makes it happen in a way we're not expecting—as if he wants to surprise us." They all laughed, convinced she was right.

Before falling asleep that night, Henriette repeated her prayer of gratitude: "Dear Lord, having this home to share with the poor is a great gift. May we always live together in love."

In the following weeks the three "sisters" began settling into a routine. Marie-Jeanne, risking the law each day by staying with them, cared for the elderly ladies while the others went about the city on errands of mercy. She also taught the slave children who came for catechism lessons in the afternoon. For the moment, she and everyone in the household enjoyed a peaceful interlude.

However, their happiness was soon threatened. The very first time Marie-Jeanne ventured out, she was accosted by an angry-looking woman who stopped directly in front of her, blocking her passage. "Are you the lady that lets those slave children come into your house every afternoon? I can tell you that the neighbors are very upset to see what's going on here."

For a moment, Marie-Jeanne seemed stunned, not knowing what to answer. Then, regaining her composure and giving the woman a friendly smile, she said, "How do you do? I don't believe I've had the pleasure of meeting you." She graciously extended her hand and continued, "My name is Marie-Jeanne Aliquot. And who, may I ask, are you?"

It was now the other woman's turn to be stunned. Not

wishing to seem rude, she stammered, *"Bonjour, madame.* I am Annette Duplantis."

Without missing a beat, Marie-Jeanne continued, "Mme Duplantis, I am so happy to meet you. I'll explain why these children come to our house, but first, tell me, do you live nearby?"

"Why yes, I live across the street a few doors down."

"Ah, that's why you've noticed the children. You see, until last year, they used to come to St. Claude's School for catechism when I was in charge there. However, the Carmelite nuns now own and operate it as a boarding school. You can understand why they have no time for extra hours of teaching."

"Well, I suppose so, but why have them come here? This is a residential area, and the people who live on this street are not happy about it," went on Mme Duplantis, sounding a bit less confrontational.

"I'm truly sorry to hear that," said Marie-Jeanne. Then, in an effort to gain the woman's cooperation, she added, "Perhaps you can help me convince them that it's an important cause."

"Oh, I don't think so," said the woman, taking a step backwards.

"But you're a force to be reckoned with, Mme Duplantis," said Marie-Jeanne, pursuing her goal. "The fact that you have engaged me in this exchange proves it. I know you don't realize it, but the work I do with my friends is actually helping the whole city." She smiled and placed a hand on the woman's arm. "Why don't you come have tea with us this afternoon? I want you to meet my companions. Then you'll see for yourself the many good things they do for children and for those who can't help themselves."

Later that day, Marie-Jeanne opened the front door and was surprised to see Mme Duplantis and another woman, each holding a covered basket. "This is my friend, Mme Chalon," said Mme Duplantis. "We've brought you some fresh bread and some fig preserves."

Marie-Jeanne introduced them to Henriette and Juliette,

who welcomed them. Over tea, they described their work with slaves and why they did it. By the time the sisters finished, the women recognized that their new neighbors were engaged in nothing less than corporal and spiritual works of mercy. From that day on, as good Christians, the women often brought food and clothing and at times offered money to help pay for medicines and other necessities. Thanks to the courtesy and ingenuity of Marie-Jeanne, other neighbors also began helping them.

On another occasion, Marie-Jeanne met an elderly black man who seemed to be staggering. As she drew closer she saw that he was trembling as if from weakness. She asked him if he was lost.

"Yes'm. I be's lookin' for Sister Henriette. I's sick and folks say she he'ps old slaves."

"She certainly does," said Marie-Jeanne, taking his arm to support him. "Come with me; I'll take you to her."

By the time they arrived at the house the old man was on the verge of collapsing. Henriette quickly prepared him a cup of tea and some bread and jam to give him strength. He revived enough to ask for shelter. The sisters could never refuse anyone in need, but since all the bedrooms in the little house were occupied, Marie-Jeanne offered to give up her own room.

"I've been here too long already," she said, "and it's dangerous for me to stay. I'll go to the Ursulines for a while. After that, I'm going to Mobile to join the Visitation Sisters— if they'll accept me."

"Dear Marie-Jeanne, we all wish you didn't have to leave us. But you're right, it is dangerous," said Henriette. "Some of the neighbors have become friends, but others have made threats. If even one of them denounces us to the police we'd all be put in prison."

Marie-Jeanne was deeply saddened. These were her dearest friends, whose work she wanted to share, but she could not continue risking their safety by breaking the law against

mixed races living together. "I don't understand," said Marie-
Jeanne, choking back tears. "I was so sure God wanted me to
work with the slaves. Now he seems to be putting obstacles in
my path."

"It's the start of a new chapter for all of us, Marie-Jeanne,"
said Henriette, embracing her. "Always remember our motto:
'One heart and one soul.' That will remind you that you're
still one of us."

No sooner had Marie-Jeanne left the society than
Henriette received word that her mother had fallen and
broken several ribs. She hurried to her side to find that
in addition to broken ribs Pouponne was suffering from
pneumonia. Faithful Nanou was there beside her, attentive
to her every need, and Dr. Briand gave her a strong sedative
to lessen the pain. After several days, Jean came from the
country and Father Rousselon came to give Pouponne
the last rites, which comforted her but did not improve
her condition. A week later, with Jean, Henriette, and her
grandchildren at her bedside, Pouponne, age sixty-three,
breathed her last.

Henriette and Jean, on friendlier terms since he had seen that
Henriette had never neglected their mother, settled Pouponne's
will. He had learned from Nanou that Henriette came to see her
mother and spend time with her every day even though she was
deeply involved with her community work. Nanou would finish
out her days with Antoinette, who had loved the elderly woman
since babyhood and was only too happy to take their beloved
slave into her own family. As for Betsy, Henriette decided to
entrust her to Jean while still retaining ownership.

When the estate had been settled Henriette returned to
the business needs of her little community. She reminded
Father Rousselon about the man now living in their house.
"Father, I think Juliette and I have to leave so the dwelling
can become an official haven for the poor elderly. The
society will, of course, continue to care for them. Don't
you agree?"

"Yes, I do," he said. "In fact, I believe this latest development is opportune."

"Why is that, Father?" she asked.

"Because just yesterday, I noticed a house for sale on Bayou Road. It looks to be in poor condition but big enough for several people. We need to find the money to pay for it so you can have your own place to live."

"I agree," replied Henriette, her smile brightening, "and I know how we can finance it."

"You always come up with a solution. What do you have in mind this time, Henriette?"

"I still have some money left me by Cécile and now an inheritance from my mother's estate. Juliette also has a small inheritance and before she left, Marie-Jeanne told us we could always count on her for financial support. I'm sure she'll make up the difference if necessary."

"That may be enough to buy the house and make basic repairs without going into debt."

Within a few weeks, all the transactions had been made and the act of sale soon followed. Having moved into larger quarters, Henriette was now certain that others would join them.

Two days later Joséphine, looking triumphant, came with startling news. "I'm coming to live with you."

"You mean your parents have consented?" cried Henriette, thrilled at this announcement.

"No, and they won't. But I've made up my mind to join you without their consent."

The two of them stared at her in stunned silence.

"I have a plan, but I need your help," she told them, her eyes sparkling. "My parents will be at the theatre tonight so they won't be there to stop me. I can be here before midnight."

Henriette and Juliette were amazed at how bold Joséphine had become. In their joyful eagerness, they immediately agreed to be her accomplices.

"We'll help you carry your things," suggested Juliette.

"Oh, could you do that? I'd be so grateful! It's not safe to walk through the Quarter alone at night."

"Of course we will," said Henriette, "and I'll ask Samuel to come with us. He'll be glad to help."

"Samuel to the rescue once again," laughed Juliette. "No one will dare harm us with him to protect us."

Joséphine exclaimed, "What good friends you are! I'm sorry to disobey my parents but they leave me no choice."

"You're obeying a higher authority, Joséphine. God's call is more important," Henriette reassured her, thinking of Jean's accusation regarding her own family ties.

At nine o'clock that night they came with Samuel to meet Joséphine. The four of them stealthily wended their way from Joséphine's home toward the house on Bayou Road, the sisters exhilarated by the idea that their collusion in this clandestine adventure was helping them achieve their goal. Shielded by the cover of night, four silent figures laden with bundles silently stole through the Quarter, unobserved, until they passed the Blue Moon, a noisy bar on Bourbon Street. At that moment a drunken sailor stumbled out, bumping into Henriette.

"Who's this? Why hello, missy," he said, taking her by the arm. "How about coming with me for a drink?" Henriette stiffened and turned to her frightened companions. "Oh, you got friends with you? How many?" he said, leering at Juliette and Joséphine.

The three of them shrank back as Samuel stepped from the shadows, allowing his massive body to tower over the startled sailor. At the sight of this menacing hulk, his lewd smile vanished and the sailor dropped Henriette's arm. Quickly he turned and stumbled back into the dimly lit tavern. The conspirators regrouped, followed by Samuel, their guardian angel, and continued their trek through the dimly lit streets. They arrived at their safe haven on Bayou Road without further incident.

Within a few days it became apparent that Joséphine's

parents would not try to reclaim their daughter. Her overriding commitment had finally convinced them of her sincerity and they agreed to allow her departure.

Even though the three dedicated companions were now united, they missed their staunch friend and supporter, Marie-Jeanne. Her absence left a large hole in their midst. Henriette in particular missed her exuberant companion, remembering how they had worked together from the beginning—ever since her dramatic plunge into the Mississippi. The sisters prayed daily for her to find peace in whatever vocation God willed.

At the Visitation Convent, Marie-Jeanne tried hard to adapt to the hours of prayer, spiritual reading, and meditation. In spite of her sincere efforts, she felt that her life had come to a standstill. After months of spiritual dryness and frustration, she knew without a doubt that the Visitation Convent was not her true calling. One day, Henriette received the following letter:

February 24, 1849
Aurelie Plantation
Jefferson Parish, Louisiana

My dearest Henriette,

When I left you back in New Orleans it was with a heavy heart. Since I couldn't be part of your community, I thought that by joining the Sisters of the Visitation I could best help the slaves by praying for them. Indeed, I did not cease praying from the day I entered, but I sorely missed seeing the children. I had no choice but to leave.

It is now three months since I came here to Aurelie Plantation, where I spend my days teaching, the work I love and am best cut out for. You are wise, Henriette: caring for the slave children is as important as praying for them. I am now certain this is my true calling.

Next week a wagon will come to your house loaded with fall crops from this year's harvest. You'll find bags of rice, yams, dried field peas, and several cans of cane syrup. I was able to get a side of bacon and some pork sausages too. We had an abundant crop of pecans that fell from the trees, which you can use to make Christmas treats for the old folks: pralines, *pain-patate,* and *crêpes* to go with the syrup. Finally, there are some bundles of cane stalks, sweeter than honey, for the children. I know how generous you are to the poor so I must beg you not to give everything away. Do keep some of these things for yourselves.

I miss you very much but know that we are bound to each other in doing God's holy will. You are all in my prayers every day.

Your sister in Christ,
Marie-Jeanne

True to her prediction, a wagonload of food arrived the following week. After that, Marie-Jeanne often sent wagonloads of fruits and vegetables according to the season, along with articles of clothing, blankets, household goods, and whatever she could gather for her friends back in the city. She knew how much was needed to carry on work with the poor. The sisters were grateful and realized that this was Marie-Jeanne's way of solidifying her ties with them.

Months passed. As expected, several women came to Mère Henriette, as she was now called, asking to join the society. At first, all were welcome, but soon Henriette realized that the mere desire to do good was not a clear indication of a calling from God. New recruits invariably expressed great enthusiasm, but once they saw how difficult the life was, they left one by one.

Henriette's desire to live for God never wavered, even in the face of great obstacles. She realized God's goodness in giving her loyal companions who remained by her side with steadfast faith. She prayed for discernment in recognizing the signs of a true vocation and began scrutinizing applicants for their determination and their vision of the austere life they would be leading.

As years passed, the community counted thirteen dedicated women. Still, Henriette's dream had not been fully realized. She wanted an official religious order with a recognized rule and nuns who publicly professed vows of poverty, chastity, and obedience. In other words, she wanted a religious order approved by Rome.

Chapter 12

From St. Michael's to First Vows

1850-1851

It was a cool, sunny day in November 1850 when Henriette and Juliette prepared for their first trip outside New Orleans. A spirit of adventure filled their hearts as Joséphine and the other sisters helped them with their carpetbags, telling them how much they were going to miss them. They all embraced with tears and hugs when the archbishop's carriage drew up in front of their Bayou Road home.

Two weeks earlier Father Rousselon had arrived with a message that Archbishop Blanc wished to see Henriette as soon as possible. "You'll like what he has to tell you. Hurry on over there."

When she arrived at Archbishop Blanc's office, he met her with a smile, saying, "Henriette, I have good news for you, something Father Rousselon and I have been trying to arrange for a long time." He motioned her to a chair, enjoying the look of anticipation on her face. "How long have you and Juliette and your companions been living together as a community?" he asked. "Almost nine years, is it?"

"Yes, Excellency, about that long," she answered, a spark of hope lighting her eyes.

"Well, Father Rousselon and I think it's time for you and your sisters to enter a further stage in your mission." He paused as Henriette sat up straighter, an expectant look on her face. "I've finally heard from Mother Annette Praz, the superior of the Sacred Heart nuns at St. Michael's. She is ready to welcome you and Juliette immediately into their novitiate program. There, by living in a formal religious community, you will deepen your spiritual formation. When you return you will be able to form your own novices, teaching them to live the consecrated life of vowed religious."

Several moments passed as Henriette took in this great news. Then a smile that the archbishop had not seen in a long time lit her face. "Oh, Excellency, I can't tell you how long we've been praying for this. This is the answer to our prayers. Just wait till I tell Juliette and the others. Now they'll surely know God wants us to be a real religious order."

"Yes, I'm sure he does, Henriette. This will give you the training you need and prepare you for the final phase of achieving your goal."

"We'll start getting ready today, but how will we get there? How far is St. Michael's?" In her excitement Henriette's mind was running ahead, anticipating the fulfillment of this long-desired goal.

He smiled. "Don't worry, Henriette. My carriage will take you there. It's a rough ride and will take about half a day, but I have no fears. You and Juliette are used to much worse trials than a carriage ride to St. Michael's.

"Mother Praz will welcome you warmly but will treat you as any other postulant. I know you've been living in community with your sisters for some time and following regular spiritual practices." He paused a moment. "And of course, nothing will ever be said about this publicly; it will be strictly between Mother Praz, Father Rousselon, and myself."

"I understand, Excellency. We don't want the authorities to find out about our going to St. Michael's. No one will know anything except members of our own community."

The following two weeks sped by, filled with preparations for their leave-taking and instructions for their absence. Finally, setting out in the archbishop's carriage, Henriette felt like pinching herself to make sure all of this was really happening.

"Oh, Juliette," she cried as she squeezed her companion's hand, "can you believe that we're really on our way?"

"I know, it feels like a wonderful dream. But suppose they don't like us? Or they think we're not prepared for the novitiate?" Juliette's joy was shadowed by a tinge of apprehension.

Henriette laid a hand on her arm and looking directly at her said, "I know how you feel; I've been worried too. But Archbishop Blanc assured me that we are well prepared and that the nuns will welcome us warmly. Mother Praz knows we've lived in community for years and already practice many of the things the nuns themselves do."

"And many they don't, I bet," retorted Juliette with a laugh.

They found the trip to St. Michael's a bit rough but not overly long or tiring. Part of the way the road was little more than a dirt path and dust from the horses' hooves kept them coughing much of the time.

The November air was becoming colder as they approached St. Michael's, near the little town of Convent, Louisiana, on the banks of the Mississippi River. They were looking forward to getting indoors and out of the weather. A middle-aged nun greeted them at the entrance and ushered them into a dark and dreary-looking parlor. The first thing they noticed was that the temperature inside was no warmer than outside. And the room had no fireplace.

Mother Praz soon appeared and greeted them graciously. "My dears, we are so happy that Archbishop Blanc was able to arrange this. He has told me all about you and your wonderful work. He said he doesn't know what he would do without you. And, we will do all we can to prepare you for your future."

Henriette and Juliette were overcome by Mother Praz's greeting. They smiled nervously and quickly took a seat on a stiff settee opposite the superior.

She looked intently at both of them then nodded her head. "The archbishop was sure you could have entered a religious order for white women with no difficulty. And now that I see you I'm sure he was right. I admire your determination to found an order for black women and help educate your own people. As I'm sure you know, we do the best we can here at St. Michael's to bring the word of God to the slaves and poor free people of color in our own community."

"Yes, Mother. Archbishop Blanc has told us of your work. We're very grateful to be here," Henriette quickly responded.

"Our house is not grand, as you can see," Mother Praz said, waving her hand around the room with its bare floor and whitewashed walls; hard, wooden furniture; and flickering oil lamps. "You'll be following the same regimen as our regular novices. They work hard and attend morning prayers with the rest of us."

Henriette and Juliette nodded enthusiastically.

"I hope the work will not be too hard for you. Archbishop Blanc informs me that you come from families of some means." She cocked her head at them, inquiringly.

"Oh, I'm sure we can do whatever you ask of us, Mother," said Henriette. Juliette nodded in agreement.

"I must warn you that some of our novices don't stay the course. They find the regimen too difficult. If at any time you wish to speak with me about any difficulties, do not hesitate. I'll understand."

"We believe it's God's will that we're here. We want to learn all we can from the good sisters of the Sacred Heart," Henriette assured her.

Mother Praz smiled. "Tomorrow when we have our chapter assembly after breakfast I'll introduce you to our community."

The two newcomers threw themselves into their duties, sweeping and scrubbing floors, washing clothes, tending kettles in the kitchen, dusting the chapel. They rose at 4:30 A.M. for the morning prayers and observed the sacred silence after night prayer. Mother Praz quickly realized that Henriette and Juliette were adapting to the community's regimen much more quickly than the younger novices usually did. She saw that they also developed a special rapport with the slaves who worked at St. Michael's, both in the house and in the fields. The area in which Henriette and Juliette had the most difficulty was garden duty. Coming as they did from the city they had no experience in encouraging the growth of herbs and vegetables and many a day Henriette left her hoeing and digging chores with chapped and bleeding hands. Juliette fared better but like Henriette found this duty the most difficult of all.

After some weeks at St. Michael's, Mother Praz called them to her office for a consultation. She informed them that she had had no complaints from the novice mistress about their service and invited them to confide in her their impression of life at St. Michael's.

They were enthusiastic in their response and complained about nothing. Mother Praz looked at them for a few moments, a thin smile creasing her lips. "I don't believe either of you is especially fitted for work in the garden. Is that true?"

"Oh, Mother, we're just not used to it. We'll do better, you'll see," they assured her.

"I know you're very willing. However, several of the nuns have observed how well received you are by the women who work in the kitchen and the fields. It's their children we teach on Saturday mornings, you know." She lowered her voice in a conspiratorial manner. "We teach them the truths of our faith, but we also teach them to read and write. This, as you know, is against the law, but their mothers, of course, can't read so are not able to teach them. I understand from Archbishop Blanc that you and your ladies do the same in New Orleans. Is that right?"

"Yes, Mother," replied Henriette. "But it's so difficult these days. We have to be very careful."

Mother Praz nodded. She was silent for a few moments. Then she said, "It has occurred to me that because of your experience, you might like to teach these children on Saturdays. We don't normally allow our postulants to do that, but you are so well qualified. What do you think?"

Oh," cried Henriette, "Juliette and I would like more than

anything to teach the little ones. We would be happy to have this additional duty."

"Then we'll make that part of your regimen starting this Saturday. And," the superior added with a smile, "we'll relieve you of garden duty."

"Thank you, Mother," they replied, beaming with joyful relief.

"Before you go there's something else I'd like to mention. We have a small but very adequate library here at St. Michael's. So, tell me, what might your favorite spiritual reading be?"

Henriette responded immediately. "Father Rousselon kindly lent me the writings of St. Teresa of Avila and I love them. I have read them over and over. So has Juliette," she said, looking over at her companion. "And of course, we've both read the *Confessions* of St. Augustine. In fact, we've tried to use the rule of St. Augustine as our model."

Mother Praz raised her eyebrows. "You've made very good choices, my dear." She looked at Juliette inquiringly. "And is St. Teresa your favorite spiritual writer also?"

Juliette hesitated a moment. "Of course I like St. Teresa very much, but my favorite reading for prayer is St. Francis de Sales—especially *Introduction to the Devout Life.*"

"Ah," said Mother Praz. "It's one of my favorites also. Do you have a copy with you?"

Juliette looked down and blushed. "No, I don't, Mother. I meant to take it but at the last minute I forgot."

"Well then, I shall lend you mine," said Mother with a smile. "I'll leave it on your bed later today."

As the winter grew fiercer, Henriette and Juliette suffered much from the cold, as did all the residents of St. Michael's. But their health remained strong and they gradually became accustomed to the chanting of the early-morning prayers, though it was not till midmorning that their feet began to thaw out.

One Saturday when Henriette and Juliette were getting ready for their catechism class with the slave children, Mother Praz intercepted them, a troubled frown on her brow. "Sisters,

I've canceled today's class. Two of our little ones have come down with a fever and we don't know whether it's contagious. We'll have to wait and see. Sister Louise, our infirmarian is looking after them."

Henriette and Juliette were disappointed for their favorite duty of the week was teaching the children. It brought back strong memories of their home and their work in New Orleans. They knew their time at St. Michael's was important because they were learning so much, but they sorely missed their own community.

Mother Praz approached them the following day after mass. She had a worried look on her face. "I told you yesterday about the two children who have come down with fever," she began. "Sister Louise doesn't think it's yellow fever—too late in the season for that—but she's puzzled about what else it could be. More than a cold, perhaps pneumonia, or possibly some other pestilential ailment." She paused a moment. "Archbishop Blanc told me that you both have done a great deal of nursing. I wondered if you would visit the children and give us your opinion."

Henriette and Juliette looked at one another and nodded. "We'll do anything to help, Mother. But what does the doctor say?" inquired Henriette.

Mother looked at them a few moments then shook her head sadly. "My dears, you don't understand. We may be able to get a doctor to come to St. Michael's for one of our nuns, but seldom will they come for a slave child. We do the best we can to care for them ourselves. Most of us are from elsewhere and are not familiar with the illnesses in Louisiana."

"Well, where are the children, Mother? When can we see them?"

"We can go right now," she replied and led them to an outbuilding next to the kitchen, not far from the herb and vegetable garden.

Sister Elodie met them at the entrance and ushered them into the makeshift sickroom holding two cots on which the children lay covered with several layers of blankets. Even so, they were shivering and a congested rattling emanated from their chests. Henriette and Juliette immediately went to them, felt their heads, and asked if they had vomited or had diarrhea. Sister shook her head but whispered that they refused to eat anything and had slept little because of the coughing.

One of the children opened her eyes and when she saw Henriette, her lips upturned a little in a tired smile, and she tried to lift her hand to touch her. Henriette quickly smiled back and lifted her head, cradling her in her arms. She kissed her on the forehead, took her handkerchief, and wiped her face. The little girl relaxed but soon began to cough again, a dry hacking sound. As if on cue, the child in the other cot began to cough too, the same hacking sound.

After a few minutes Henriette gently propped the girl's head higher on the pillow and rose to speak to Mother Praz. "If they were sick with malaria or cholera or some other pestilence, by now they would be having much worse symptoms," she whispered. "They either have pneumonia or some other bad lung condition." She advised remedies she had learned from her mother: a hot chest compress soaked in camphor oil and a tonic of honey and chamomile tea. And broth, of course, if they could keep it down.

"Juliette and I will be happy to nurse them, Mother, if we can be excused from our other duties," she offered.

"I would be so grateful," Mother Praz replied instantly. "And you're sure it's not some contagious pestilence?"

"Well, I don't think so. Do you, Juliette?"

Juliette shook her head vigorously. "No, the signs are not there."

Henriette and Juliette devoted themselves to nursing the two children, Amos and Odile, and after a few days they began to show some signs of improvement though they remained very weak. It was some time before they were strong enough to join the Saturday catechism class again.

Meanwhile, Henriette and Juliette described to Mother

Praz the symptoms of various pestilences—yellow fever, cholera, smallpox—that regularly ravaged New Orleans and the surrounding areas. In France, from where most of the Sacred Heart sisters had come, they knew little of such plagues. However, the superior had heard enough of them to be fearful for her community.

Mother Praz thanked Henriette and Juliette publicly at one of the community meetings and asked them to tell everyone of their work with the sick and elderly in New Orleans. Henriette spoke simply and forthrightly of the ministry of her little group, describing their nursing of yellow fever and cholera victims as well as the frail and disabled elderly, many of whom they had rescued from the streets of the city.

"Why are they in the streets?" asked the novice mistress.

Henriette hesitated. "Well, Sister, sometimes when a slave is too old or too sick and weak to work, the family that owns them . . . Well, if they can't take care of them, they just put them out on the street to beg for a living."

This caused quite a stir among the nuns, some of them sucking in their breath, raising their eyebrows, or shaking their heads sadly.

"Did I understand correctly that you also have taken responsibility for the burial of some slaves?" interjected Mother Praz at one point.

"Yes, Mother, sometimes we've had to do that. And when we weren't able to get the service of a priest we said the prayers for the dead ourselves. Father Rousselon said it was all right."

"Of course, my dear," said Mother Praz softly. "We are all in awe. We simply have not had such experiences, but we admire your faith and your courage."

As the months passed, Henriette and Juliette grew more and more anxious to return to their own community. One day early in autumn, Mother Praz summoned them to her office.

"I know you are eager to return to your own home," she said with a smile, "and I'm quite satisfied that you've learned all you need in order to complete the formation of your new order of women religious. I might add that you have taught all of us a great deal, too, dear Henriette and Juliette."

The two blushed and then expressed their thanks to Mother Praz for her hospitality, patience, and instruction in religious formation as well as her interest in their own community.

Mother Praz started to say something, then stopped. Finally she said, "I hope you won't mind my asking you this. It's been on my mind for some time. What is your opinion of slavery? I believe you yourself own a slave, Henriette. Is that true?"

"Yes, Mother. Actually, there have been two slaves in our family for a long time. Old Nanou, who passed away a year ago, was like a second mother to me; and there's Betsy, who was left me by my sister, Cécile, now living with Cécile's daughter. In my will I have left her to my brother, Jean. As for slavery, I'm sure I speak for Juliette and for all of our sisters at home: we think it is an abomination and most displeasing to God."

"Why then do you keep a slave, my dear?"

"For one thing, Betsy is not like most slaves. She and Nanou were always like one of the family. But mainly now it's so difficult to free a slave. Betsy would have to leave the state because that's the law. But where would she go? She'd rather stay with our family—as a slave it's true, but more like one of us."

"Ah, I understand now. You see, you've taught me something else."

She looked at the two women with fond eyes. "I hate to see you go. I wish more than anything that you could stay with us. But, of course, that's not why you came."

The following week Archbishop Blanc's carriage arrived to take them back to New Orleans. Mother Praz and many of the community were on hand to see them off. And just before they boarded, two little children ran up from behind the nuns and handed Henriette and Juliette a big bouquet of yellow chrysanthemums. They were Odile and Amos.

The sun was setting when the bishop's carriage pulled up to the house on Bayou Road. As Henriette and Juliette climbed down from the high seats, the sisters, who had been waiting all day, ran to greet their beloved founders. Overjoyed to see each other after such a prolonged absence, they hugged and laughed and cried, saying over and over again, "Welcome home. Welcome home."

"We've missed you so much," Joséphine said, wiping her eyes.

"We missed you too, dear Joséphine, all of you," said Henriette. "We're so happy to be back. And look who's here," she cried, catching sight of Marie-Jeanne Aliquot.

"Yes, she's come from the plantation just to welcome you home," said Joséphine. "And that's not all." She turned to a young woman standing just behind her, took her hand, and drew her forward. "We have a surprise for you, Mère Henriette. Here is a newcomer to our house, Suzanne Navarre, come all the way from New York to join us!"

"How wonderful," exclaimed Henriette, taking both the woman's hands in hers. "Suzanne, what a lovely name. You're the first person from outside of New Orleans to join us. I must hear all about how you learned of us and why you came."

And so they continued exchanging expressions of loving friendship as they trooped inside, until Joséphine suddenly remembered they had promised to fetch Father Rousselon when the wayfarers arrived. She quickly ran the short distance to St. Augustine Church to return with their beloved pastor.

"Oh, Father," cried Henriette when he arrived. "I can't wait to tell you how much we've learned."

"Don't even try," he replied, laughing, "at least not this evening. I wanted to welcome you home and to give you my blessing. This is the beginning of a big new step for all of you."

Just then Joséphine announced imperiously, "We have a nice big pot of gumbo waiting in the kitchen. I can't believe no one's hungry."

They all laughed, then prayed grace, and tried to remember the last time they had enjoyed anything as delicious as a steaming bowl of shrimp and okra gumbo.

In the ensuing days, Henriette drew up a daily schedule

based on the ancient monastic rule of *ora, labora, et lectio*—prayer, work, and reading—similar to the one she and Juliette had followed at St. Michael's. Only after faithfully living under the rule and observing the vows of poverty, chastity, and obedience could they apply for official status under Rome. When she had it worked out she presented it to Father Rousselon for his comments before introducing it to the community.

"This looks fine, Henriette. Now tell me how you will manage instruction concerning the vows. There is a big difference between those who have been with you from the beginning and the newest members."

Henriette nodded in agreement. "At St. Michael's we learned the seriousness of taking vows, so I think it best if I explain to the original members how this step will affect our lives. In the meantime, Juliette will teach the postulants the basic principles of the religious life, starting with proper decorum."

"Good thinking, Henriette," said Father Rousselon, smiling. "Get them off to the right start. I remember when I taught new seminarians they couldn't chatter all the time and that they had to avoid being loud or boisterous."

Henriette laughed when she explained that new recruits at St. Michael's were amazed at having to walk, talk, and even laugh in a manner befitting a dignified religious.

"Well, Henriette, I don't think you've left a single stone unturned," chuckled Father Rousselon. "And of course, as always, the rest of your day will be devoted to the spiritual and corporal works of mercy."

"Father, I pray that we may soon have our little community operating with one heart and one soul, like a close-knit family."

"That gives me another idea, Henriette. I've been thinking about a name for your community and you've just given me an idea. What would you think of calling yourselves the Sisters of the Holy Family?"

Henriette's eyes brightened. "Sisters of the Holy Family!" she repeated. Hearing the name stirred her to the core. In a flash, she saw that by pursuing God's will, she had enfolded her mother, brother, and relatives into a new and better family relationship. "Oh, Father, I like it very much. In fact, I think it's perfect."

"So be it then. From now on that's what you'll be: the Sisters of the Holy Family."

Chapter 13

Bold Adventures

The weeks passed quickly as Henriette and Juliette instructed Joséphine, Suzanne, and the others in the regimen of the spiritual life as practiced by the sisters at St. Michael's. Enthusiastically, they took to the program, except for the sacred silence, which they all found difficult. There were so many things to talk about at the end of the day: little slave children who posed amusing questions, ailing slaves who trusted them implicitly, destitute and abandoned blacks in need of care or burying, and, of course, the continuing ill will and insults from some of their own *gens de couleur*.

Henriette assigned duties by the week. "Suzanne, you and Joséphine will tend the sick this week. The new patient who arrived a few days ago complaining of stomach pains seems to be doing better. It was probably from eating tainted food."

"Yes, Mère Henriette, now that we've moved the sick to the brick building behind us, we have more time to care for them," replied Suzanne.

"Juliette, I'd like you to work with Régine, visiting those families who lost loved ones last summer during the cholera epidemic," Henriette continued. "I seem to remember the Rideau family was especially hard hit."

"And Lorraine, you come with me. We need to comb the Quarter to find some decent clothing for the new orphans we've acquired."

After their daily chores two of the sisters taught catechism to the slave children. It was gratifying to see

the pews at St. Augustine's gradually fill up with young
people practicing the faith they learned as children from
the sisters' religious instruction.

Though none of the sisters grumbled or complained
about their work, there was one activity that everyone agreed
was the most difficult of all: begging. Some Creole families
were generous; others often discharged them with rudeness
and insults, even slamming the door in their faces.

One evening during the recreation hour, someone asked
Margot, the newest member of the community, how she was
adjusting to this unpleasant task.

"To tell the truth, I find it distasteful to ask for money and
at times even frightening," she answered hesitantly.

"My dear, we all know how you feel," sympathized
Henriette. "We need to remind ourselves to put our feelings
aside when asking for alms."

"I know we're asking for the poor," replied Margot, "but
when someone shouts at me, my heart starts pounding and I
want to run away."

"Suzanne, tell her about the time you and Paulette went to the
house on Barracks Street. That ought to give her some courage."

They all turned to Suzanne as she recalled the day she
and another sister went begging and a big burly man with a
huge moustache opened the door. He glowered at them and
shouted, "Who are you, dressed in those ridiculous outfits?
You masquerade in those dark skirts and bonnets as do-
gooders but I've seen you dragging along with drunken men
in the backstreets. I suppose you want money to buy more
liquor. Get away from my door before I send for the police!"

At this, Margot raised her hands to her face in horror and
squealed, "Oh, Sister, I would have fainted on the spot."

"Most of us would," agreed Juliette, "but Suzanne held her
ground. Go on, Suzanne, I didn't mean to interrupt."

Suzanne admitted that on previous occasions such an
outburst would have sent her scurrying, but this time she
held her ground. "I knew his accusations were ridiculous,"
she continued, "so I looked him straight in the eye and said,

'Sir, you are mistaken. We are Sisters of the Holy Family. You may have seen us leading a sick slave to a safe place so he wouldn't die in the street.'"

"What did he say to that?" asked Margot, wide-eyed.

"At first he didn't say anything, then he screamed at us again, 'What do you care if some slave dies in the street? Why do you have to make it your business?' I suddenly felt very bold," Suzanne continued, "and answered him right back. 'Sir, it is our business because Jesus told us, "Whatever you do to these the least of my brethren, you do to me."'"

"Good heavens, that must have gotten his attention," said Margot, on the edge of her seat. "What happened then?"

"He stared at us, grumbled under his breath, and slammed the door. Just as we turned to go down the steps, he reopened the door and threw something at us."

"What was it?" Margot asked in alarm.

Suzanne smiled back at her. "A crisp new five-dollar bill!"

Everyone laughed heartily and told Margot that since then they frequently asked God to bless the "big burly man with the booming voice."

There were days when the sisters returned empty-handed from their begging trips. If there was food in the house, they gave it to those in greatest need, eating little themselves or simply drinking a glass of sugared water for supper.

One such evening when Sister Nadine learned there was nothing to prepare for their own supper, she burst into tears and ran out the back door so the others wouldn't see her. Hidden in a far corner of the courtyard she gave vent to bitter tears. "Oh, God," she prayed, "I'm so hungry and so tired! Dear Lord, how do you expect us to do your work if we don't even have food to eat?" In desperation she sobbed, "If we don't get something to eat tonight, I can't stay here another day. Do you want me to stay or don't you?"

She was still weeping when she heard a clatter inside the house as if they were being invaded, followed by loud laughter and exuberant chatter. "How can they laugh at a time like this?" she groaned aloud to herself. As the hubbub from within continued, and fearing she might be missed, Nadine dried her eyes and went inside. All the sisters were milling about the kitchen, opening boxes and gunny sacks and piling the glorious contents high on the table.

"Oh, Sister Nadine, come and see what our darling Marie-Jeanne has sent us from the country. Mère Henriette said she knew all along it was coming but didn't know exactly when it would arrive. She didn't tell us because she wanted us to be surprised."

Nadine's eyes widened as she beheld a vision too good to be true: mounds of yams, pole beans, okra, Creole tomatoes, zucchini, summer squash, ears of corn, and cans of syrup, sacks of pecans, and a lovely string of sausages.

Before she could take it all in, Sister Nadine felt a huge lump in her throat and tears of gratitude welling in her eyes. "O dear God," she said half under her breath, "I guess you want me to stay after all."

"I heard that, Nadine. Very funny!" laughed Sister Corinne. "As if you'd ever consider leaving us."

A rueful smile played about Nadine's face. She turned aside and prayed, "Thank you, dear Lord. We won't go to bed hungry tonight."

Despite ongoing hardships, the little community continued its mission. Gradually the intense spiritual regimen became their normal lifestyle.

One morning after mass, Father Rousselon drew Henriette aside and said, "Henriette, I think the time has come for you to take your first vows."

"At last! I don't have to tell you how happy this makes me."

"Is there anyone else you think might be ready?" he asked, smiling.

"Yes. Juliette and Joséphine. They have been with me since the beginning."

"You understand, of course, that they will be private vows until such time as your community receives formal Church recognition."

"Yes, Father, and now I'm sure that day will come."

On October 15, 1852, the community gathered before Father Rousselon at St. Augustine's to witness the simple ceremony as Mother Henriette Delille, Sister Juliette Gaudin, and Sister Joséphine Charles knelt and pronounced their dedication according to the formula: "I vow and promise to almighty God to live the rest of my life in poverty, chastity, and obedience, according to the rule of St. Augustine."

On that day, their hearts were filled with joy. After the mass of celebration, the community gathered together in the parlor to congratulate them. Each of the sisters gave them a little gift—a beautiful holy card, a medal, a small crucifix—whatever they had to mark this special occasion. Father Rousselon gave each of them a bound French missal, which he had ordered from Lyon.

Prominent in the thoughts of the newly vowed religious was the memory of Sister Ste Marthe, the beloved teacher of their childhood, the one who, more than any other, had influenced them to follow this path by her own example. They could not help thinking how proud she would be of her former students. Though she had never returned from France, her loving influence was still deep within their hearts.

In the ensuing days each of the sisters redoubled her efforts to live the religious life as perfectly as possible in preparation for the day when she would pronounce her own holy vows. The sisters grew increasingly used to the life of a religious, which was becoming more organized, settled, and peaceful.

Henriette found that she had time to think about her personal affairs. Now seemed the right moment to revise her own will and perhaps change the destiny of Betsy. Since returning to New Orleans from St. Michael's, she had given much thought to Betsy's future, prompted probably by the questions of Mother Praz about owning slaves.

One day when Juliette returned from visiting the sick, Henriette took her into her confidence. "Do you remember Mother Praz asking us how it was we could own slaves?"

"Yes, of course."

"What do you think, Juliette? Is it right?"

Juliette frowned and after a few moments shook her head.

"I don't know, Henriette. I don't own a slave so I haven't thought about it. But I think what you told Mother Praz is true. Many slaves are almost members of the family, like Betsy and Nanou were to you and Cécile."

They were silent for a few moments.

"You know, I've talked to Betsy and she would like her freedom, but she doesn't want to leave. She would have to go somewhere else, leave the state. I don't know what to do. I think slavery is wrong because for one person to own another is treating them almost like an animal or a piece of property."

"Yes, I agree. So many people suffer because of it. How can it not be a sin in God's eyes?"

"But I heard Father Rousselon talking to one of the church wardens the other day—they had been reading a newspaper from up north denouncing slavery—and Father didn't say it was wrong. He seemed to agree with the warden that if slaves were treated properly it was perfectly all right with God."

Juliette frowned again. "I don't know what to think. What can we do about it anyway?"

"Well, I'm revising my will. In that will I made last year when I was so sick, I left Betsy to Jean. I'm a little worried though. You know, Jean has been in the business of buying and selling slaves, something he knows I don't approve of. I don't think he would ever sell Betsy if he owned her, but . . . I'm not certain of that."

"Oh, Henriette, you're much younger than Jean, and you're well now. Why are you thinking these things?" Juliette raised her eyebrows then asked anxiously, "You are well, aren't you?"

"I'm fine." Henriette laughed. "It's just that it's a good thing to get one's life in order, and for the first time since getting back from St. Michael's, I've had time to think about it."

They sat in silence again, questions quietly whirling around their hearts.

"Henriette," Juliette broke the silence, "coming back to what Father Rousselon said. That bothers me. Are you sure you heard him right?"

"Yes, I'm sure."

Juliette frowned and shook her head. "I think that it must be a sin in God's eyes. But for some reason good people, even very good people like Father Rousselon, don't think so. Perhaps one day they will."

After a time Juliette spoke again. "So, what about Betsy? What are you going to do?"

Henriette sighed. "I think I have to say in my will that I wish to free Betsy. I'll insist that she stay in service to Jean until such time as she can be freed without leaving the state."

"That's a good idea."

Just a few days after this conversation Henriette and Juliette discovered that there were other ways for slaves to find their freedom—but not without great risk. When they heard a loud knock on their door late one night they thought someone was coming with an appeal for help. Henriette opened the door and saw before her two women dressed quite properly with dark scarves shrouding their faces. Before she could greet them, the smaller woman moved inside, pulling her companion with her. She tossed aside the scarf and revealed her identity—to everyone's delight.

"Oh, what a good surprise, Marie-Jeanne! I thought it might be you," cried Henriette as she hugged her dear friend. "And who is this with you?" she continued, looking at the other woman, who seemed to hang back. "You are both most welcome."

Marie-Jeanne gently pulled her companion forward and removed her scarf. Standing before them was a lovely young woman of fair complexion with a cascade of brown curls framing her face. Most striking were her huge hazel eyes, made brilliant by flecks of green and gold. But she was obviously nervous and upset, looking around her with a frightened expression. Her brow was furrowed in an anxious frown.

"What's the matter?" Henriette asked. "Come, sit down, both of you. Juliette, fix us some tea, would you? Have you had supper?" Juliette gave her a sharp glance, for there was very little in the larder that day.

"Don't worry, we're fine," replied Marie-Jeanne. "My friend

Titia is a little frightened because we have embarked on an unusual adventure and we've come to ask your help."

Henriette looked at Marie-Jeanne, her brows raised in question. "My dear, you know we will do anything we can to help you."

Marie-Jeanne turned to the frightened young woman and led her to the center of the room for all to see. She wore a lovely light green dress and a shawl of multicolored thread. "My friend Titia needs to stay with you for a few days," she said, looking at them with a serious expression. "Is that all right?"

"What do you mean?" Henriette replied. "You know you're always welcome, but we take a chance every time we go against the law."

Marie-Jeanne smiled reassuringly. "I do know, but it will only be for a short time. Let's have our tea and we'll tell you all about Titia and our plans for her escape," she paused a moment, looking around at all of them, "from her slave master."

Juliette almost dropped the tea kettle as she and Henriette gasped, realizing for the first time that not only was Marie-Jeanne's companion black but that she was a fugitive slave. "What are you saying?" Henriette finally managed to ask. "Do you realize this is even more dangerous than having you stay with us?"

"Yes, of course I do, but it was the only plan I could come up with."

Turning to Titia, she said, "Tell these good friends of mine where you're from, my dear, and how long you've been at the plantation."

Titia looked nervous, glanced at Marie-Jeanne for encouragement, and then slowly told her story. "Ah bin . . ." she began slowly, as though coached in her delivery, and then said, "I have been at Beau Rivière Plantation since I be's . . . since I was ten years old. I came from Aurélie Plantation where I were . . . was born. I was changed to Beau Rivière Plantation. I am a housemaid. Mah mistress, she die . . . died las' year . . . so I nursemaid Mars' li'l chirren. Then . . ." She became confused and looked again at Marie-Jeanne pleadingly.

"That's all right, Titia. I'll tell them. I'm afraid that Titia's story is one that's all too common in this slave owners' society of ours.

As you can see, Titia is a most attractive octoroon and becoming the mistress of a rich white owner wouldn't be unusual. But Titia is a good Catholic girl and knows that would be wrong." Marie-Jeanne paused and smiled at Titia then leaned over and patted her on the arm. Henriette and Juliette sat on the edge of their chairs as their longtime friend told her story.

"Titia was separated from her family when the master of Aurélie Plantation exchanged her for a young boy slave from Beau Rivière. She kept in touch with her two brothers at Aurélie, always hoping to rejoin them. Recently the new master has begun making advances. Titia detests him and fears him because of his cruelty. He often beats his slaves and once hanged a runaway slave to teach them all a lesson."

"Hanged him? Dear God, that's unthinkable!" cried Juliette in disbelief. "The man's a monster."

"I can't blame her for wanting to escape," added Joséphine, deeply moved.

"Yes, you're beginning to understand," said Marie-Jeanne, continuing her story. "Titia managed to get word to her brothers, who told me they wanted to somehow rescue her. We've devised a plan that will work, but I need your help."

Henriette leaned forward and asked, "How did you manage to get her here?"

"Well, as you know, I come to New Orleans often to visit Sister François at the Ursuline Convent," she explained. "This time, before leaving the plantation, I arranged with Titia's brothers to bring her to a certain wooded area where I met them. From there, Titia rode to New Orleans with me."

"And what about the two brothers?" inquired Suzanne.

"They're back on the plantation. It's much too risky for the three of them to escape together."

Everyone nodded in agreement. They had all listened in wonderment as Marie-Jeanne told of her bold escapade but, understandably, were fearful of its ultimate outcome. Finally, Henriette uttered what they were all thinking: "But Marie-Jeanne, what will you do with her? Where will she go? Maybe we can hide her here for a few days, but what then? There will be notices all over the countryside and in the city as well. All the newspapers will carry news of a runaway slave from Beau Rivière."

"I've thought of that and here's my plan. Sister François wrote to an old friend of hers at the Sacred Heart Convent in St. Louis, Missouri. Those nuns have a school for the Potawatomi Indians in Oklahoma."

"Oklahoma?" cried Suzanne. "Where's that?"

"Somewhere around Texas," replied Marie-Jeanne. "My sister has requested that her friend take in Titia then send her to the Indian mission. She'll be a great help there. She's smart. The Sacred Heart nuns might even get her all the way to California. No one could possibly find her there."

They looked at Marie-Jeanne in astonishment.

"As soon as Sister François hears from her friend, we'll book passage for Titia on a boat to St. Louis. My biggest problem is finding a suitable chaperone to travel with her. She cannot go alone. I think it would be preferable if it were a man."

No one spoke a word as Marie-Jeanne looked around at all of them.

"It's entirely too dangerous," said Henriette finally.

Marie-Jeanne retorted, "Listen, all of you: God did not save me from a watery death for nothing. Helping Titia is the least I can do and I know God will provide. Henriette, look at how he has provided for you. Did you ever think you would be able to have your own house, to take vows as religious, to be the shining light that you are in this godless city?"

They were all quiet for several moments. Suddenly the silence was broken by the sound of muffled sobs from Titia, who was all but forgotten in a corner of the room. They crowded around her, assuring her that all would be well, that she was in good hands, and that God himself was guiding them.

"Don't worry," Henriette assured her. "You'll stay with us for a while—you'll be safe here—until word comes that you can go to find your freedom with the Sacred Heart sisters in . . . in . . ."

She looked at Marie-Jeanne, who smiled and added, "In Oklahoma."

Henriette wisely added, "Marie-Jeanne, I think it would be

safer if Titia stays with us while you stay with Sister François at the Ursulines."

"I couldn't agree more," said Marie-Jeanne, "much safer indeed."

As it turned out Titia stayed hidden in their house for many days. Finally, after almost two weeks, word came that the Sacred Heart nuns would be thrilled to welcome Titia and send her on to their mission in Oklahoma. A ship was scheduled to depart soon afterward for St. Louis and Sister François booked passage for Titia immediately.

"God is indeed guiding us," she told the Sisters of the Holy Family. "I've found a chaperone for Titia. One of the Ursulines has a brother visiting here from Philadelphia. He's sailing up to St. Louis on business and has agreed to accompany Titia on the trip."

Having satisfied herself that the gentleman in question was trustworthy, Marie-Jeanne confided to him that her young friend was extremely shy, having grown up in the country. She told him not to be surprised if she spoke seldom and in a very soft voice with a strange accent. Marie-Jeanne headed back to Aurélie Plantation almost immediately after the necessary plans had been laid, prepared to tell wonderful stories of her visit with Sister François and news of what was happening in the big city.

For weeks after Titia's flight, Henriette and her nuns prayed fervently and offered their daily sacrifices for the safety of Marie-Jeanne's young charge. They were all greatly relieved and had a joyous celebration when they heard from Marie-Jeanne's sister that their bold adventure had come to a good conclusion. Titia was indeed safe in the St. Louis convent and would soon be journeying on to the unfamiliar territory of Oklahoma.

In the following months and years Henriette and her sisters spoke often of that dangerous yet exhilarating period in which they became the instruments of freedom for a fellow human being caught in the evil bond of slavery. Though most of their good works were not so daring, they were numerous and dramatic enough to eventually merit the respect and good will of many of the *gens de couleur* and the white community in New Orleans.

Chapter 14

The Spirit's Guidance

1861

On the morning of April 21, a well-dressed young woman knocked on the door at 72 Bayou Road asking to see Mère Henriette. The woman introduced herself as Béatrice Bonard and said she was interested in joining the Sisters of the Holy Family. Henriette had learned by experience to be wary of accepting everyone who came knocking on her door. She tried to distinguish those with a true calling from those merely seeking security or companionship. On past occasions eager young women had joined the sisters only to discover that the life was simply too difficult to endure. Henriette doubted that this stylish young woman was ready to beg in the streets or care for dying slaves. Nonetheless, she greeted Miss Bonard politely, then came right to the point.

"What makes you think you have a religious calling?" she asked.

"Well, I'm not sure our Lord is calling me, Mère Henriette, but I've been wanting to speak to you for some time." The young woman hesitated then added, "It's because of what happened to me last winter."

"Yes? Please go on."

"Well, one day in February, I saw a man lying on the sidewalk in broad daylight. He looked terrible and I thought he was drunk. He was all curled up and was shaking from head to toe. His clothes were filthy and his hair was long and matted. I crossed the street to get away from him but couldn't help staring all the same."

"Were you frightened?"

"Yes, but mostly I was disgusted and didn't want to be seen near him. Then I saw two women dressed in black coming toward the man. I thought they, too, would cross the street to avoid him, but they went right up to him."

"What happened then?" prompted Henriette, becoming more interested.

"I was shocked to see them stoop down and speak to the man. They took turns stroking his head, pushing the dirty hair from his face, and helping him to sit up. After struggling for some minutes, they managed to get him on his feet. One of the women took off her shawl and put it around his shoulders. Then they slowly led him back down the street to where they had come."

"Who were those women?" asked Henriette, already knowing the answer.

"That's what I was wondering until a passerby told me they were Sisters of the Holy Family. She said they often pick up sick and abandoned slaves."

"Have you seen any of our sisters since then?" Henriette wanted to know.

"Yes. Coming out of church one day, I saw the same two nuns and couldn't help asking them what had happened to that man. They told me he died of pneumonia a few days later."

"That was old Ruben," said Henriette, "a slave who belonged to a family in the Marigny. Years ago he used to pull a little wagon selling okra which he grew behind the slave cottage. When all the okra had been sold, neighborhood children would climb into his wagon and he'd pull them all around the Quarter. He was very kind to them."

"Why, I remember seeing that man but had no idea it was the same person I saw lying in the street."

"Surely that one incident isn't what makes you want to join us?" asked Henriette, still skeptical.

"But it is, Mère Henriette. I can't get that scene out of my mind, and I feel terribly guilty about having misjudged that old man. When I saw the sisters treating him so kindly, I felt like the Pharisee in the Gospel who passed by the man lying in a ditch. I feel as if this is our Lord's way of telling me I should make amends. If I join the sisters and undertake the same work, wouldn't that set things right?"

"Perhaps, Mlle Bonard, but I think we need to give it more time. I want you to pray daily to the Holy Spirit for guidance. I'll do the same. Come back in three months and we'll talk again."

Henriette recognized a deep sensitivity in the young woman but wondered whether she could adjust to putting up with long hours of backbreaking work often undertaken in dank, unhealthy quarters amidst ill-smelling sick people. Perhaps she would be like the rich young man in the Gospel who wanted to follow Jesus but couldn't bring himself to give up his wealth. She breathed a prayer that if it was God's will he would guide Béatrice back to them.

For the time being, Henriette had other concerns which occupied her thoughts. Every day people in the streets were talking about war and President Lincoln's desire to abolish slavery. White Southerners felt threatened.

"Who will do the menial work if there are no slaves?" asked the city dwellers.

"Lincoln's insane!" scoffed the plantation owners. "Giving up slavery is out of the question."

And warmongers everywhere were screaming, "Every man, woman, and child is ready to fight to defend our way of life!"

It seemed to Henriette that men and boys of every age were ready to take up arms. Political leaders threatened to secede from the Union. Thank goodness poor old Nanou had passed on, but Betsy, still young and strong, had asked Antoinette, "Where will I live? Who'll take care of me if I be free?"

Henriette learned from Joséphine that her parents, like most free people of color, had a different outlook. They hoped the Emancipation Proclamation would take effect. "We'll finally be free of those unjust Louisiana laws," her father told her. "Why, we'll even be able to vote."

Free people of color were convinced that their education

and cultural refinement put them on an equal footing with upper-class white Creoles. Henriette's nephew, Samuel, once told her, "Everyone can see that the *gens de couleur* are superior to brutish Americans, especially the likes of those 'Kaintucks.' As for the businessmen, do you think they care about us? All they care about is making money."

Henriette pondered these questions and concluded that whatever the political outcome or whoever came to power, her community's objectives would remain fixed. Since she and her nuns had often been treated with disdain, it was not discrimination she feared, but war. War meant fighting, killing, maiming—leaving families both black and white devastated for generations, bitter with resentment, and bearing scars of hatred and vengeance. These issues weighed heavily on her soul.

In the midst of her pondering, Henriette was surprised by the sudden appearance of Juliette. "Henriette, I thought you had a visitor here with you."

"I did, Juliette, but she left some time ago. A lovely young woman named Béatrice Bonard. She's thinking of joining us."

"Well, what do you think? Will she fit in?"

"I'm not sure. She seemed completely candid so I asked her to come back in three months. Keep her in your prayers. If she really has a vocation, I think she'll pursue it with all sincerity and good will. Just think, Juliette, that would bring our total number up to fifteen."

"I can hardly believe it. After so many have left, it seems we're finally beginning to get solid vocations. I will pray for Miss Bonard."

"Where are you off to, Juliette?"

"It's almost four o'clock. I'm just leaving to meet the children for catechism class. They're making their First Communion in two weeks, May 5 to be exact. Why don't you come with me? The children would love to see you."

"I think I will come and say a few words to them. I promised some time ago I'd visit before the end of the term."

When the two of them arrived at the school, several

children were frolicking about on the banquette, laughing and chasing each other. Upon seeing the nuns they ran to greet them with smiles and hugs.

"Mère Henriette, you seen dem soldiers marchin' in da square?" asked little Joshua. "Dey be wearin' gray suits and caps to match."

"And dey all got guns," added Henri, his eyes wide with excitement.

Henriette's face fell. She stood silent for several moments. She finally asked, "When did you see them marching?"

"Dey be marchin' now. Da white folk say da ships blowed canons at Fort Sumter. Dey say dat now we be's in war. But it don't feel no diffen' den befo'."

"Children, those things are way off in South Carolina," said Juliette, hastening to reassure them. "It's very far from here."

Henriette's worst fears were realized. She suddenly felt the energy drain out of her. After a long moment, she heard Juliette's voice as if from far away.

"Come inside, children. Mère Henriette came to visit your class today. She has some important things to tell you."

That evening the nuns learned that there had indeed been an official declaration of war. Henriette felt not only physically exhausted but depressed, thinking of the suffering war would bring in its wake. Seeing how wrenching the news had been for Henriette, Juliette urged her to retire early. The fact that she accepted this advice without objection confirmed Juliette's suspicions. Henriette was not well.

Though not really old, forty-eight on her last birthday, Henriette felt her body wearing out. She tried to ignore the increasing difficulty in rising each morning at 4:30. Some days her muscles and joints were racked with pain from too much physical activity the day before and too little sleep at night. The worse she felt physically, the more she begged Jesus to give her strength to continue his work. Her most impassioned prayers were for the future of the fledgling community.

In the morning Henriette still felt fatigued and was

breathing heavily. She nonetheless resumed her daily round of prayer and work.

Within weeks of the declaration of war, the city was in confusion. White people expected to be protected by the Confederate soldiers. Black people, on the other hand, looked to the Unionists to abolish slavery. At Sunday mass, Father Rousselon told the people to pray that the Confederate army would protect the city.

Later, in private, he said to the nuns, "Most people don't realize that there could be out and out rebellion. Bloodshed would be everywhere from an uprising of slaves against their masters. That's how it happened in Saint Domingue."

The Sisters of the Holy Family tried their best to maintain an atmosphere of normalcy in the community and among the children. They taught their classes and ministered to those in need, in spite of dwindling resources.

Henriette was surprised when one day in September she had another visit from Mlle Bonard. Though more than three months had passed since their first visit, she had not stopped praying for the young woman, thinking that perhaps Béatrice had changed her mind about joining them. Yet here she was, standing before her with shining eyes.

"Mlle Bonard, how nice to see you again," she said, greeting her with enthusiasm.

"Hello, Mère Henriette. I know you must have given up on me, but so many things have happened that I couldn't get back to see you. I don't know where to begin telling you everything."

"Why don't we begin by sitting down?" invited Henriette, directing her to an armchair near the window. "Now, just begin where you left off. I assume you've been praying for the Holy Spirit's guidance?"

"Yes, I have, Mère Henriette. And now I'm certain God is calling me."

"How so?" said Henriette, a little bewildered.

"You see, Mère Henriette, when I first spoke to you, I wasn't really free to join you. But now I am."

"I don't understand. You weren't free then, but you are now?"

"Yes, because my protector was alive then, but no longer."

"Your protector? You mean . . ." Henriette's eyes widened as she realized what Béatrice was telling her.

"Yes, I think you can guess. Several years ago my mother formed an alliance for me with a white Creole gentleman. He was kind and attentive at first but often drank too much. I was very unhappy. I never really wanted this alliance, but my mother insisted. She said I would never find a free person of color who could provide for my future as he could."

"I understand," said Henriette. "Please continue."

"After M. Bienvenue—that was his name—joined the army, he was seriously wounded, so General Hood sent him back to New Orleans. He lingered for a time but his wounds were very serious and the journey had been hard on him. He died a few weeks ago. Since then, I've realized that these events have been providential. Now I'm convinced that God is calling me."

"I see." Henriette paused, not quite sure how to proceed. "Tell me, were there no children from this alliance?"

"Yes, five years ago we had a son but he died shortly after birth. That's when M. Bienvenue stopped coming to see me."

"And how have you been managing all this time?" asked Henriette.

"He gave me the house I live in and continued sending me a monthly allowance."

"So, since he hadn't cut you off, you knew he might return to claim his rights over you," reasoned Henriette.

"Exactly! Every day was agony not knowing when he might show up."

"Yes, I can imagine," said Henriette, rising and taking a few steps, "but what of your mother? She must have been a comfort to you in your distress."

"My mother died three years ago. If she were still alive I would have been less lonely these last years. As it was, I felt useless and abandoned. My mother, my child, and my protector, all gone."

"You know, Béatrice, loneliness is not necessarily the sign

of a true vocation. Many people are lonely, but it doesn't mean God is calling them to religious life. You could marry if you're seeking companionship."

Beatrice smiled and looked into Henriette's eyes as she answered. "I know that. But it's more than just loneliness. Something inside hurts when all around me I see people suffering. God has shown me how much love you offer to the poor and the sick. I want to be of service to them—like you and your nuns."

Henriette was silent for a moment. "Tell me, did you see M. Bienvenue before he died?"

"Yes, I did," she responded. "One day there was a knock at my door. When I opened it I saw two bedraggled soldiers supporting a third between them. It was none other than M. Bienvenue. He was half dead and I was horrified at the sight of his bloodstained bandages. I resented that he had come back to me instead of to his legal wife. Later I learned he sent his wife to France before the war began."

"So, did you turn him away?" asked Henriette.

"No, that's the surprising thing. For some reason, the memory of old Ruben lying on the sidewalk flashed through my mind. I remembered how my revulsion disappeared when I saw your sisters treating him with such kindness. At that moment, my feelings toward M. Bienvenue changed and I was able to put aside my resentment and care for him—just as I had seen your sisters treat old Ruben."

"Oh, Béatrice, that was a wonderful act of kindness. God's grace was surely working within you."

"I've always dreaded the sight of blood, and yet I was able to dress his wounds and comfort him."

Henriette was impressed but cautious. "Are you sure you can live as we do? It's not an easy life. Many have tried and have left because they found it too difficult. You especially, Beatrice; you're accustomed to living in relative luxury. Can you really give up all the comforts you've known?"

"I'd willingly give them up to be useful. Won't you please let me try?" Beatrice begged.

Henriette felt the young woman's sincerity. "It certainly seems that past events have led you to our door. When do you think you'd like to join us?"

Béatrice was ready for this question and answered resolutely. "As soon as I can sell my house. I'll put the money in escrow. If my calling is not of God, I'll be able to return to the world. If it is, the money will go to the Sisters of the Holy Family when I die."

"I see you've given this a lot of thought. Very well, Béatrice, let me know when your financial matters are settled and then we shall open our doors to you."

"I don't know how to thank you, Mère Henriette."

By Christmas, the young woman had managed to sell her property and put her affairs in order. Early in the new year she stood smiling, a small suitcase in hand, at the sisters' door: "Here I am, Mère Henriette, come to join you."

"Welcome to the Sisters of the Holy Family, Béatrice Bonard," Henriette said, returning her smile. "Come in and meet the community."

From the first day of her entry, Béatrice felt in her heart that she had made the right decision. As the weeks and months passed, she became increasingly convinced that there her life had meaning. There she could make a difference. She was content.

Henriette began coughing a great deal in March but did not seem to have a cold. In the following days she had several more coughing spells which shook her entire frame. To soothe Henriette's throat, Juliette prepared a special honey and lemon drink for her. By April the cough was better but had not disappeared.

"Henriette, you're looking very tired lately," Juliette remarked. "Why don't we get Dr. Briand to come take a look at you?"

"I am a bit tired, but as soon as this cough is gone, I'll be fine," said Henriette, dismissing the idea with a wave of her hand. "Let's wait and see before we bother Dr. Briand."

Chapter 15

Now Thou Dost
Dismiss Thy Servant

1862

Though still only a postulant, Béatrice showed tremendous good will and complete obedience to everything asked of her. Henriette was thrilled at these signs of a true vocation, knowing that if Béatrice persevered she would be a valuable asset to the community, and prayed, "Thank you, dear Lord. If you send us more like Béatrice, I'll feel better about our future, in spite of the war."

By mid-May, Henriette seemed to be better and went on a begging tour of the Marigny with Béatrice. As they turned into Frenchmen Street, however, Béatrice looked apprehensive.

"Mère Henriette, must we stop at the first house on this block?"

"Why, yes. We stop at every house. Is there some reason not to stop here?"

"The woman who lives here was a friend of my mother's. I haven't seen her since the funeral and she has no idea that I've joined the sisterhood," Béatrice said. "I'm afraid she'll be rather shocked to see me begging."

"I see. But we don't beg for ourselves, Béatrice," said Henriette sympathetically. "We're doing this for God's poor. You knock. I'll ask the Holy Spirit to give this lady an understanding heart."

Summoning her courage, Béatrice knocked firmly at the front door of the attractive Creole cottage. It soon opened to reveal an elegant middle-aged woman who seemed both pleased and confused as she recognized her deceased friend's daughter.

"Why, Béatrice, is it you?" she said, looking confused as her eyes swept up and down the postulant's somber dress. Quickly regaining her composure, she added, "How nice to see you again." Then, aware of Henriette, she said, "Won't you and your friend please come in? It's very warm outside for this time of year."

"Thank you, Mme Girod. I'd like to present Mère Henriette, foundress of the Sisters of the Holy Family," said Béatrice.

"I'm happy to meet you, Mère Henriette."

After they were seated she turned to Henriette and said, "I've heard good things about your work with the yellow fever victims."

"Our community does minister to them, but we try to help the poor and the sick wherever we find them. The war is making our work more difficult and that's the reason we're here today requesting alms for the poor."

"We?" she said, turning to the younger woman. "Am I to understand that you are begging, Beatrice?"

"Yes, Mme Girod. I've become a member of Mère Henriette's community. This is the dress worn by new postulants."

"I see. I must say I'm surprised. And what would your mother have said of this?"

"I don't think she'd be opposed. Once she saw the problems caused by my alliance with M. Bienvenue, she realized what a mistake the arrangement had been. She'd be happy to see me spending my life where I can find fulfillment."

"Well, when you put it that way, I think I see your point. People are doing all kinds of unexpected things these days since this terrible war started. Nothing is the way it used to be, especially since that Yankee, General Butler, took over our city."

Suddenly all three women were startled by raucous voices shouting curses in the street. Rising to look out the front window they saw a group of Yankee soldiers shaking their fists at a woman standing on a second-story balcony holding aloft an empty chamber pot.

Mme Girod's expression turned hard as she added, "Right there! That's a perfect example of what I mean."

Henriette shook her head and said, "I've heard of people doing these things, but it's not the way to solve our problems."

"You have to understand, Mère Henriette, people hate the Yankees. Women especially are resentful of General Butler, who encourages his soldiers to come in and help themselves to all the silver in our homes. And his cruelty is beyond belief. He's threatening to put women in jail for offenses far less outrageous than what you've just witnessed."

"How unfortunate. Cruelty just makes people more bitter," uttered Henriette, who seemed overcome by the entire scene.

"He does as he pleases. He's guided by savage instincts. His latest proclamation forbids the use of the French language!"

Henriette and Béatrice both looked incredulous. "But surely people will speak whatever language they wish," countered Béatrice.

"You may think so, but he's clever. Starting Monday, all classes in the public schools must be taught in English. And that's not all," continued Mme Girod. "The most despicable ordinance to date is a promise of freedom and money to any slave who reports that his master has hidden arms. He's destroying our whole society."

"O dear God, where will all this end?" breathed Henriette.

By this time Mme Girod was becoming completely unstrung. "Why, the latest news I heard just this morning is that one of Marie Laveau's protégées has put a voodoo curse on the Beast. That's what they call him."

At this news, Henriette was so taken aback that she began coughing violently and had to sit down again. Mme Girod hurried to bring her a glass of water but it was some time before the spasms subsided. Breathing normally again, Henriette suggested to Béatrice that they return home since she was feeling a bit faint.

Before they left, Mme Girod reminded them that they had come asking for alms. Offering them a packet of bills she said with apologies, "I'm sorry I can't be as generous as I would like; Confederate dollars are all I have. Thanks to that Devil of Dixie, our money is almost worthless." The two nuns thanked their hostess and rose to leave. "I hope I haven't upset you too much with all this talk of the war, Mère Henriette. Please come back when you're feeling better, and Béatrice you must come too."

Béatrice was frightened at seeing Henriette looking so pale and exhausted. She helped her down the front steps and arm in arm they slowly returned to the house on Bayou Road. It was many days before Henriette was able to resume any regular activities.

News of the war, along with the Yankee occupation, weighed heavily on the citizens of New Orleans, on the nuns, and especially on Henriette, who felt responsible for the whole community. By early summer the entire city was suffering from food shortages. The best produce in the market was preempted by the Yankee soldiers, who let the townspeople scrounge for whatever was left behind. Sprouted yams, bruised fruits, and spoiled vegetables became their daily fare. Coffee was scarce and had to be stretched with far more chicory than usual. Henriette began visibly losing weight. Her usually quick step slackened as she virtually dragged her tired legs around the Quarter on her rounds. The torrid days of July stretched into the steamy month of August and there was no letup in the insults and deprivations resulting from the Yankee presence. By the time September arrived, Henriette felt discouraged, not only because of her declining health, but because three of the younger nuns had left the community. Living the strict religious rule in the hostile environment of New Orleans proved beyond their capabilities. She thanked God for her faithful followers who persevered in the face of adversity, among whom she still counted Béatrice.

Speaking to her one morning Henriette said, "Béatrice, I'm encouraged by your perseverance. The fact that you're still here, my dear, in spite of all our hardships, convinces me of your calling."

The younger woman was silent for a moment, then looking at Henriette she said, "At times, it is more difficult than I had imagined, but when I think of how much our soldiers are suffering, I offer the hardships to God and beg him to end the war and give us peace."

Henriette was grateful for Béatrice and for all of her staunch followers: Juliette, her childhood friend and companion, and Joséphine, who had risked being disowned by her family. They never flinched from doing work that most people would not consider undertaking. Dear Suzanne had come all the way from New York to join this new community founded to help slaves. And last but not least, her constant helper in time of need, though absent by necessity, faithful Marie-Jeanne, always assisting Henriette any way she could. These had been with her from the beginning. Combined with the few she had left—twelve in all—Henriette was convinced that the Sisters of the Holy Family would survive regardless of what happened to her.

One bright day as she and Juliette were passing St. Louis Cemetery #2, she surprised her companion with an unusual request: "Let's stop here. I want to ask the caretaker if there are any available tombs. It's always a good idea to be prepared for the future."

Juliette, suspicious of what her friend was thinking but not wishing to contradict, agreed with what seemed a normal reaction. "If you wish. In fact, why don't we both talk to the caretaker? After all, I'm older than you and will probably precede you to the grave."

And so they did, each having made a momentous purchase before they left the premises. Realizing, however, that Henriette's health was worse than she had let on to the community, Juliette resolved to send for Dr. Briand that very day. When he laid eyes on Henriette and heard her cough, he feared the worst.

"Henriette, I know how responsible you feel toward your charges, but you must stop work until you're rid of that cough. I'm prescribing special medicine and complete rest."

"Complete rest." Those words sounded so inviting to Henriette. For a brief moment she thought of letting go of her responsibilities. Then, as she remembered the suffering of people around the city, she replied, "Dr. Briand, I can't possibly stop all my work, but I'll try to cut back on the number of hours."

"Then I can't promise you will get well," he said, shaking his head sadly.

In the ensuing days she did try to curtail her work load, but unable to put her own needs ahead of others, she spent each day working until her strength gave out. In late October she was forced to take to her bed. The sisters visited her each day, praying fervently for the recovery of their dear Mère Henriette. Even as she grew weaker, she saved enough strength to welcome each of her friends in turn.

Having heard the news of Mère Henriette's illness, Marie-Jeanne came in from the country. "My dear child," she said, holding Henriette's hand, "you've exhausted yourself doing God's work. But we're asking him to restore your health and give you back to us. We need you so much."

Though burning with fever, Henriette smiled at her longtime friend and benefactor. "Dearest Marie-Jeanne, do you think God will send someone to fish me out of this sick bed as he fished you out of the Mississippi?"

Marie-Jeanne's eyes were brimming with tears as she answered, "None of us knows the future, but I know it was he who fished me out, as you say, and put us together. It's been the greatest blessing of my life to have known you and worked with you."

Juliette cared for and comforted their beloved founder. "Henriette, I've made you a little broth. Won't you try and swallow some?"

Henriette smiled and nodded. "If you made it, of course I will." Juliette helped her to a sitting position and propped her up with several pillows. "Juliette, I want you to know that when I pass, you must carry on. And I'm leaving my personal possessions to you. It's in my will."

Juliette dreaded losing Henriette, her dearest childhood friend. Shy, quiet Juliette knew the rest of the community would expect her to fill Henriette's shoes, but she also knew that no one could replace Henriette. It was just a matter of time until the inevitable happened.

Whenever Béatrice popped her head in, it cheered Henriette. She felt a special kinship with this younger woman who, like herself, had overcome social barriers to follow her own instincts.

"How is it going for you, Béatrice?" Henriette wanted to know.

"Oh, Mère, I can't tell you how happy I am to be where I feel useful," she answered with a broad smile.

"I hope you'll always keep this sunny disposition, Béatrice. But surely you must feel discouraged sometimes, don't you?"

"When I find myself tempted to complain or feel sorry for myself," explained Béatrice, tilting her head slightly, "I just remember how unhappy I was before, and then I feel grateful to be where I am."

"Your cheerfulness reminds all of us to smile in spite of difficulties," said Henriette. She knew that if Béatrice maintained this positive attitude, she would persevere to final vows.

Finally, Father Rousselon was called to anoint Henriette with the sacred oils of extreme unction. From his first day in New Orleans when she had befriended him, he had admired her intrepid spirit and unflinching dedication. Seeing her so wasted shocked him with the possibility of losing her. It would be a great loss, not only to him personally, but to her community and to the entire city.

All the sisters gathered around her bed to pray with him in the anointing of the sick. Father Rousselon tried to encourage Henriette with thoughts of recovery. "You know, Henriette, the sacrament of extreme unction often has a healing effect. I'll pray very hard that God will make you well again so you can continue to serve him. You're still young and there's much work to be done."

"Thank you, Father. You're so kind," whispered Henriette. "But I think God wishes me to work from another place. Please continue supporting our little community as you always have. Our greatest wish is to have Rome approve our rule."

"Of course, Henriette. You know I'll do whatever is in my power to fulfill that wish."

Upon hearing this promise from her faithful friend, she released her concerns for the future of the Sisters of the Holy Family. In the silence of her heart, she gratefully repeated her favorite prayer: "I believe in God. I hope in God. I love. I want to live and die for God."

Father Rousselon and the sisters stayed kneeling by her bed for a long while after the anointing. Henriette smiled wanly at them before drifting into a peaceful sleep. As he left, Father Rousselon asked Juliette to inform him of any change in Henriette's condition.

October slipped away and fused with the cooler days of November. Around the middle of the month Henriette rallied slightly. Juliette reminded her that November 21, the anniversary of their humble beginnings as the Sisters of the Presentation, was fast approaching.

Henriette nodded and said, "You and Joséphine will have to celebrate without me."

"Why, Henriette, you'll be right here with us to celebrate. And now that you're a bit stronger, perhaps you can even come downstairs and we'll celebrate with the whole community."

But it was not to be. Henriette's intuition had been accurate. She died quietly on November 17, days before that memorable Feast of the Presentation of Our Lady.

"Now she will celebrate in heaven," said Juliette. And Joséphine agreed. Together they wept over their terrible loss.

St. Augustine Church was crowded with people from all over the city and all levels of society who came to pay their last respects to this saintly woman, known by everyone as Mère Henriette. Among the mourners were Henriette's niece and nephew, Antoinette and Samuel. They would never forget the loving care she had always shown them. Her brother, Jean, also assisted at the final rites. Since their disagreement years earlier, he had come to admire Henriette's stubborn conviction that God was leading her. His regret for having judged her harshly was replaced by pride for his courageous and generous little sister. Conspicuous by their absence were her closest family members who had preceded her in death—Pouponne, Cécile, and their dear Uncle Félix. It was he who first recognized Henriette's rebellious spirit against pressure from her mother, her family, and society in order to improve the lives of black people.

A few days after the funeral, the following obituary appeared in the daily *Courrier.*

Last Monday there died one of those women whose obscure and retired life has nothing remarkable in the eyes of the world, but is full of merit before God. Miss Henriette Delille had for long years consecrated herself totally to God without reservation to the instruction of the ignorant and principally to the slave. To perpetuate this kind of apostolate, so different yet so necessary, she had founded with the help of certain pious persons the House of the Holy Family, a house poor and little known except by the poor and the young, and which for the past ten or twelve years has produced, quietly, a considerable good which will continue. Having never heard of philanthropy, this poor maid has done more than the great philanthropists with their systems so brilliant yet so vain. Worn out by work, she died at the age of fifty years after a long and painful illness borne with the most edifying resignation. The crowd gathered for her funeral testified by its sorrow how keenly felt was the loss of her who for the love of Jesus Christ had made herself the humble servant of slaves.

Epilogue

With the Civil War still raging in the country after the death of their beloved founder, the Sisters of the Holy Family found themselves in an arduous struggle for survival. Within six months, they also lost their beloved friend and benefactor, Marie-Jeanne Aliquot, to pneumonia. Soon some of the newest recruits, unable to cope with the intense privations and suffering resulting from the war, began leaving the community. The remaining few stalwart members depended on Juliette and Joséphine to guide them through what must have seemed like the dark valley of death.

Near the close of the war in 1864, the Sisters of the Holy Family, like the South in general, was reeling in the social confusion resulting from the abolition of slavery. This situation was most difficult for the sisters since slaves were the main focus of their mission. Nevertheless, clinging to the vision of their founder, they continued to teach all black children who came to their school, whether former slaves or *gens de couleur libres.*

Through years of trial and struggle, the community again began to grow in number and to be recognized beyond the confines of the French Quarter for its charitable works. In 1870 the community was able to acquire property on Chartres Street formerly used for the trading of slaves. Abandoned by the city as a place of injustice and infamy, the sisters considered this disposition of the building a fitting end to the cruel story and a blessing and satisfying final chapter. It became St. Mary's School, the first high school for black girls in the United States.

In 1881 the sisters acquired the building on Orleans

Street once known as the Quadroon Ballroom. Ironically, the same building once used as an elegant dance hall where "alliances," were often formed, became the motherhouse of the congregation founded by and for free women of color. The sisters remained in the French Quarter until the 1950s, when they built their present motherhouse on Chef Menteur Boulevard. Today, the Lafon Nursing Facility of the Holy Family, a home for the elderly, as well as Saint Mary's Academy is located behind the motherhouse on this vast property.

With renewed vigor and the continuing guidance of the Holy Spirit, the Sisters of the Holy Family have spread their work throughout the state of Louisiana and beyond, to places as far away as California, the District of Columbia, Central America, and Africa. Faithful to the vision of their founder, the Sisters of the Holy Family continue to teach, nurse, and care for the least of their brethren, counting among their foundations the first home for the elderly in the United States.

At the annual meeting of American bishops in 1988, Archbishop Francis B. Schulte of New Orleans proposed Henriette Delille as the first African American saint from the United States. The appeal was unanimously accepted by the bishops and in 1989 her cause, asking that her life be examined for the purpose of beatification and canonization, was introduced in Rome.

Mère Henriette leaves an impressive legacy of dedicated religious who today constitute the largest religious community of women in Louisiana. They live with the same single-hearted commitment as the one Mère Henriette wrote in her prayer book: "I believe in God. I hope in God. I love. I want to live and die for God."

Prayer for the Beatification of Henriette Delille

O good and gracious God, you called Henriette Delille to give herself in service and in love to the slaves and the sick, to the orphan and the aged, to the forgotten and the despised. Grant that inspired by her life, we might be renewed in heart and mind. If it be your will, may she one day be raised to the honor of sainthood. By her prayers, may we live in harmony and peace. Through Jesus Christ, our Lord. Amen.

Glossary

Chapter 1
Mme: abbreviation for madame; French punctuation uses a
   period after single letters only
Pitout: pronounced Pee-too
Ah, mon cher Pitout! Oh, my darling Pitout!
Maman: Mama
calas tout chaud: warm rice cakes
calas: rice cakes
comestibles: food
Oncle: Uncle (dialogue uses French spelling, narrative uses
   English)
mulatto: offspring of one white and one black parent
beignets: deep-fried fritters similar to doughnuts
gens de couleur libres: free people of color
Pouponne: nickname for Henriette's mother, Marie
   Josephe Diaz

Chapter 2
banquette: sidewalk
Mon Dieu: Dear Lord

Chapter 3
Creole: a person of part European extraction; here, a free
   person of color
placée: placed; refers to the system of *plaçage,* also known as
   alliances

coiffeuse: hairdresser
Bonsoir. Good evening
Quelle jolie robe! What a pretty dress!
Oui, monsieur, avec plaisir. Yes, sir, with pleasure.
merci: thank you
levée: levee

Chapter 4
café au lait: coffee with milk
placer: to place

Chapter 5
tante: aunt
roux: mixture of flour and fat to thicken sauces
gumbo z'herbes: a thick gumbo made with herbs
C'est charmant! It's charming!
parquet: main floor

Chapter 6
Tiens, bonjour, mes chères. Why, good evening, my dear ladies.
five dollars: about seventy dollars in today's money
merci beaucoup: thank you very much

Chapter 7
yellow jack: yellow fever
parapluies réparés ici: umbrellas repaired here

Chapter 8
les peaux rouges: red skins; Indians
bel pam patates: lovely potatoes

Chapter 9
je ne sais pas: I don't know
bamboula: the name of an African dance
calinda: another African dance
gris-gris: a curse

Chapter 10
marraine: godmother
Au secours! Help!
holy viaticum: extreme unction, the last rites

Chapter 11
Jeanne d'Arc: Joan of Arc
pain-patate: sweet potato pie
crêpes: very thin (dessert) pancakes
mère: mother

Chapter 12
infirmarian: the person (nun) in charge of the infirmary
    (sick room)

Chapter 14
escrow: funds deposited or put aside until further notice

Chapter 15
General Butler: Benjamin Butler, the general in command of
    Union troops stationed in New Orleans